WAR DRUMS

JOHN VORNHOLT

Abridged and adapted by Joanne Suter

GLOBE FEARON
EDUCATIONAL PUBLISHER
PARAMUS, NEW JERSEY

Paramount Publishing

 Adapted from WAR DRUMS by John Vornholt, published by Pocket Books under license from Paramount Pictures.

Globe Fearon Educational Publisher, a division of Paramount Publishing, 240 Frisch Court, Paramus, New Jersey 07652.

Printed in the United States of America
1 2 3 4 5 6 7 8 9 10 99 98 97 96 95 94

ISBN: 0-835-91103-9

GLOBE FEARON
EDUCATIONAL PUBLISHER
PARAMUS, NEW JERSEY

Paramount Publishing

CONTENTS

CHARACTERS

Crew of the *U.S.S. Enterprise*

Beverly Crusher—Doctor

Data—Lieutenant Commander and android; serves as the *Enterprise*'s science officer and helmsman

Geordi La Forge—Chief Engineer

Guinan—hostess of the Ten-Forward lounge

Jean-Luc Picard—Captain

William Riker—Commander and first officer

Ensign Ro Laren—Starfleet Officer from Bajor

Deanna Troi—Counselor

Worf—Klingon Security Chief

Other characters

Balak, Turrock, and Wolm—young Klingons shipwrecked on the planet Selva and at odds with colonists of New Reykjavik

Gregg Calvert—security chief for New Reykjavik, a Federation colony on the planet Selva

Myra Calvert—twelve-year-old daughter of Gregg Calvert

Raul Oscaras—president of New Reykjavik

Dr. Louise Drayton—chief scientist on New Reykjavik

The song of the birds stopped suddenly. Three women and three men entered the circle of trees. They carried baskets, buckets, blankets, and tools. All six wore plain brown clothes and heavy boots.

Two of the women laid a blanket on the ground. They unpacked their picnic baskets. The other four carried the buckets and tools to the trees. Soon there came the sound of hammering as they worked to get the sap from the trees. The women on the blanket put out boiled eggs and sandwiches.

Suddenly the peace was broken by a wild scream. A naked figure jumped out of the trees. It landed amid the food. It was hairy, but not hairy enough to be an ape. There were ridges on the creature's forehead.

One of the women reached into her picnic basket. She pulled out a phaser. The creature knocked her down with one heavy blow. Then the Klingon, for that is plainly what it was, began to scoop up the food.

More naked Klingons came out of the woods. They screamed and leaped on the humans like a pack of wild dogs. The attack turned into a bloody battle. Captain Picard moved uneasily in his chair, but he kept his eyes on the viewscreen. He had seen Klingon violence. But nothing like this. Klingons were warriors.

They liked a good fight, but they fought by the rules. These skinny, dirty Klingons were like animals, snarling and biting.

They clearly wanted the food. As soon as the first Klingon had the picnic basket in his hands, the others tried to leave, too. One human struggled to his feet. He pulled out a phaser and shot. The smallest Klingon was hit in the back by the glowing beam. He spun and fell.

Now the scene changed. The recorded log showed the Klingon prisoner being led into a walled fort. Someone had tied a rag around his waist so he wasn't naked anymore. His young face was black and blue as if he had been beaten. The boy looked as if he expected to die, but his eyes were proud. He looked now, thought Picard, more like a Klingon than like a beast in the woods.

"End log," said a deep voice.

The lights came up in the observation room of the starship *Enterprise*. A large, bearded man stood at the front of the room. He was the same man who had fired the phaser in the log. Around the table sat Captain Picard's most trusted officers. There was First Officer Will Riker, Commander Data, Doctor Beverly Crusher, Commander Geordi La Forge, Counselor Deanna Troi, and Ensign Ro Laren. Every eye turned toward the security officer at the far end of the table, Lieutenant Worf. The big Klingon stared silently at the blank screen.

One by one, they turned away from Worf. But the man standing at the front of the room continued to stare. His eyes were filled with hate. "Lieutenant Worf," Raul Oscaras growled, "do you still deny that we are being attacked by Klingons?"

"No," Worf said through his teeth. "It is also clear that you have beaten your prisoner. Such treatment goes against all Starfleet rules."

"In the year that we have been on Selva," said Oscaras, "we have been attacked by this gang of Klingons forty-two times. They have killed eleven of us. They have wounded sixty-nine. We are afraid to leave our fort. How do you expect us to treat these beasts?"

Captain Picard held up his hand. "It won't help to argue among ourselves, Mister Oscaras."

"*President* Oscaras," the man corrected.

"President Oscaras," Picard continued. "New Reykjavik is a Federation colony. Starfleet has sent us to settle the problem. Whatever you may think of Klingons at the moment, I can promise you, those are not usual Klingons. I have never seen them act like that. The Klingons are warriors, yes. But they are proud. They do not act like wild animals."

Oscaras stared out the window at the stars. He shook his head. "I wish you could hear their drums," he whispered. "They play them all night. Our children cry. No one sleeps. We've tried to hunt them down, but they're part of the forest. They sleep in trees or dig into the ground. No matter what you say, Captain, they are animals. You must help us hunt them."

"I don't understand this," said Riker, leaning forward. "The Federation only starts colonies on empty planets. Were the Klingons there when you arrived, or did they come later?"

The big man frowned. "We scouted Selva for three years before we settled there. We found no one. But now we see how the Klingons disappear into the forest. We know they were hiding from us. For the first few months," he continued, "there was no sign of them. Then the attacks began. They stole whatever they wanted."

Picard nodded. "Then our first job is to find out where they came from." He turned to Worf. "Lieutenant, I suggest you contact Klingon High Command. Find out how these Klingons came to Selva."

"Yes, sir, right away." Worf seemed happy to leave the observation room. When the door shut behind him, Raul Oscaras leaned across the table.

"Captain Picard," he said, "I'm really not sure your Klingon can be trusted in this matter."

Jean-Luc Picard glared at his guest. "First of all, President Oscaras, he is not *my* Klingon. He is Starfleet's Klingon, and a fine member of this crew. Secondly, we may discover that the Klingons arrived on Selva *before* the settlers. In that case, *you* have gone against the Prime Directive by settling an already inhabited planet."

"We didn't know!" declared Oscaras.

Data tipped his head. "That is no excuse for breaking the law," he said.

"Heaven help me!" moaned Oscaras. "Out of all the ships in the fleet, why did they send you?" His angry eyes moved from Data to Ensign Ro. Ro could not stop herself from touching the bony ridge between her eyes. "Half the crew isn't human!" Oscaras exclaimed.

"No," replied Ensign Ro, "but we make do."

Will Riker smiled slightly. Then his face became very serious. "President Oscaras," he warned. "I wouldn't continue this line of thought."

The big man lowered his head. "We've faced these attacks for months. It's making us all a little crazy. You've got to help us."

Picard stood. "We will," he promised. "For now, return to your people. Let us look into the matter. A party will beam down in the morning."

The angry visitor left the observation lounge. Picard turned to his crew. "Data," he said, "Work with Worf. Check Starfleet records. See if there were ever missing Klingons in this area."

Geordi spoke up. "I'm going to run a scan of that planet. Maybe there are other things they don't know about."

"Ensign Ro will help you," said the captain. "Beverly, what did you think of this meeting?"

The red-haired doctor frowned. "One thing bothers me. To get that video record, they must have set up cameras. Then they brought out all that food. It was almost as if they were inviting an attack."

"They knew we were coming," said Deanna Troi. "They wanted the log for proof. I sense that Oscaras is a clever man. He may use these attacks to make his own control over the colony stronger."

Picard nodded. "Number One, you and I will go on

this away team. Counselor Troi, Dr. Crusher, and Data will join us. Usually I would say Worf. But we don't know how many others think like Oscaras. Ensign Ro, I would like you to come along."

The slim Bajoran nodded. "Thank you, sir."

"Very well," said Picard. "The away team will meet in ten hours in transporter room three."

"Get some sleep, everybody," said Doctor Crusher. "We may need our wits down there."

Worf stared at his viewscreen. He waited for the Klingon librarian to answer his questions. It seemed to be taking the fellow a long time to find the information.

"I only want reports on a few refugees," Worf muttered. "It was ten years ago. There were Romulan attacks on some colonies in this section."

"All Klingons are gone from those colonies," the librarian answered coldly.

"But what happened to the Klingons who escaped the attacks?" asked Worf. "Could they have gone to other planets in the area?"

With a scowl, the clerk replied, "Open your data channels. I am sending those records now—I would appreciate your keeping it quiet."

Worf quickly punched in the command to receive the information. He looked at Data.

"What do you expect to find?" the android asked.

"I've looked at Oscaras's log again. I guess the oldest of those Klingons to be about fifteen in Earth years. I saw no adults. The way they act, as the captain noted, is most unusual."

"Unless they were not raised by Klingons," added Data.

"Exactly," agreed Worf. "When there is a war, Klingons often send their youngest children away. Everyone else stays to fight, to the death if necessary. Knowing this, I started looking for wars that were fought in this area about ten years ago. There were, indeed, planets settled by the Klingons. But the Romulans claimed them, too, as they do most everything. The Romulans attacked again and again. At last the Klingons had to leave their settlements. But I have no reports about escape ships or refugees. It is possible that an escape ship might have reached Selva."

Data turned to the panel behind Worf. "Here, I believe, is your information."

Worf peered at the screen. "At the height of the attacks," the Klingon read aloud, "forty-eight children were sent off on a ship bound for a Klingon base. They never reached the base. No wreckage was ever found. The ship was thought to have been destroyed by the Romulans."

"I believe your idea is correct," said Data. "That ship might have reached Selva."

"The children ranged in age from babies to six years of age. That matches the ages of the Klingons in the log."

"What will the Klingons do if these are the refugees?" asked Data.

"That is hard to say," Worf answered. "Klingons do not like to remember their battle losses. They may not be happy to have the refugees found." He frowned. "I think we should wake up the captain."

Captain Picard sat on the side of his bed. He listened closely to his officers' ideas about the Klingon youths.

"These may be the missing children," he agreed. "But unless we find the ship, it's just an idea."

"Captain," said Worf, "we must talk to the prisoner. He is the key."

Picard nodded. "We're going to try to have the boy handed over to us. It's for his own safety, if nothing else."

"I know I am not going with the away team tomorrow," said Worf. "But sooner or later, someone will have to go down to that planet. Someone will have to find the Klingons. I am the best choice."

"I agree," said Picard. "But we have to see what we can expect from the settlers. Data, what rights do the Klingons have under Federation laws?"

The android tipped his head and answered, "Klingons are allies of the Federation. They have the same rights as Federation citizens. Since they were on Selva before the settlers, they cannot be forced to leave the planet. The settlers would, in fact, need their okay to be there."

Picard sighed and rubbed his eyes. "First we have to get the parties to stop killing each other. Talking sense into Oscaras and the settlers will be hard enough. How do we talk to teenagers who have grown up alone in the woods?"

"Captain," said Data, "the three of us speak Klingon. We can talk with them if they remember any of their language. We can give them communication badges with translators. Wearing the badges, they will be able to understand anyone."

Picard stood. "We have to find them and help them all we can. Lieutenant Worf, let the Klingon High Command know what is happening. Data," the captain added, "when we meet the prisoner, remember his coordinates. We want to be ready to borrow him if need be."

"It's a very young planet," Ensign Ro said. She and Lieutenant Commander Geordi La Forge were looking at charts of Selva. Ro's finger traced the earthquake fault lines that crisscrossed the planet.

"At least they picked the safest body of land," said the Bajoran. "And they're close enough to the ocean to enjoy a warmer climate. I wouldn't want to build a skyscraper down there, but my people are living in places that are far worse."

"All those springs and underwater volcanoes must keep that ocean pretty warm," said Geordi. "The water is hot, and most of the land is cold and covered with ice. I'd say they definitely picked the best spot."

"Except that there were Klingons already living there."

Geordi sighed. "I'm not sure what the captain can do

about that problem. But I'll keep checking the planet while you're down there. At least I can tell you what the weather will be like."

"This could be a difficult mission," Ro said, more to herself than to Geordi. "I'd better say good night."

The chief engineer smiled. Ro could imagine the warmth in the eyes hidden behind his VISOR. "Take care of yourself, Ensign," he said.

The Bajoran smiled. "Did you notice that I was the token bumpy-head on the away team?"

"Well," Geordi said, "they have to know that no race is alone in this universe. And you have seen how hard it is to make a home in a new world."

"Sometimes I wish the Bajora were like those Klingons," said Ro. "If we had fought like animals, maybe we wouldn't have been kicked from planet to planet." She sighed. "Good night, Commander."

Ensign Ro took the long way back to her cabin. She found herself entering the Ten-Forward lounge. The cafe was home base for her best friend on the *Enterprise*, the mysterious bartender Guinan.

Ro stood at the window. She looked at the rust-colored curve of the planet Selva below them.

"I hear you're going down there in a few hours," said a voice beside her.

Ro turned to the brightly dressed woman. "Yes," she answered, "but I can't sleep."

"Why not?" asked Guinan. "It's an easy job ahead of you—just overcome prejudice and fear."

"Right," sighed the Bajoran.

"Especially fear of the Other."

"The Other?"

"The different," said Guinan, "the unusual. The one who won't play by the same rules you do. You've been the Other all your life. Now you've got to teach people not to fear it. Ro, I have a feeling this is a special job ahead of you. I have a feeling you are really needed down there."

"Well, there's no reason I should be so nervous," said the Bajoran. "I'm sure I'll be back tomorrow to tell you all about it."

"Perhaps." Guinan smiled. "Whenever you come back, please stop by. I'm very interested."

"Good night," said Ro.

"Peaceful dreams," replied the bartender.

Six sets of dancing lights sparkled in the settlement on the planet Selva. Three men, two women, and an android appeared. One by one, Captain Picard, Commander Riker, Lieutenant Commander Data, Ensign Ro, Doctor Crusher, and Counselor Troi stepped forward.

They found themselves within a fort built to protect. Houses and buildings were all made of metal. The high walls were metal, too. They were topped with barbed wire and sharp stakes.

A child of about six or seven stared with wide eyes. "Have you come to kill the drummers?" she asked.

Will Riker knelt down. "We haven't come to kill anyone," he answered. "We've come to make peace. Isn't that better?"

"No!" She shook her head. "My daddy says there won't be peace until they're dead."

Now children and adult colonists circled the away team. All wore the same plain, brown clothing. Their eyes seemed to say, "We don't trust strangers."

Deanna Troi noticed many of the colonists staring uneasily at Ensign Ro. But the slim Bajoran paid no attention to the looks. She studied the readings on her tricorder.

President Oscaras came out of the crowd.

"Welcome!" he roared. "We can offer you food and drink, though it is all from the replicator now. The savages have made it impossible for us to plant crops or gather food from the forest. We use the replicator to make everything, including phasers."

Beverly Crusher was smiling at a little girl. "I'm a doctor," she said. "I wanted to make sure you feel all right. Do you like living here?"

"I want to go home," the girl answered. "Back to Iceland."

A red-haired woman pulled the girl away. "This is home for you. You know that."

"Actually," said a young man, "there are a lot of us who would like to go home."

His words were met with some loud boos and a few quiet cheers.

"Enough of that talk!" growled Oscaras. "The crew of the *Enterprise* didn't come to listen to our complaints or to take us back to Earth. They've come here to rid us of the beasts in the forest!"

Those words were followed by cheers from all. Picard cleared his throat. "I hate to tell you," he began, "but the Klingons have as much right to be on this planet as you do. It appears they may be refugees from a war and victims of a spaceship crash. If so, they've been here nine years longer than you have. We will try to reach them. We want to ask them to live in peace with you."

There was silence. Deanna sensed many emotions. Some people were angry. Others were confused.

At last a woman shouted to Oscaras. "You said they

would help us. They're siding with them!"

"I said I would call the Federation for help," said Oscaras. "These people don't know what we're up against. They even have a Klingon on their ship. I say let them go into the forest. They will soon learn there is no way to deal with the beasts!"

"Give us weapons!" shouted a big man. "We'll finish them off without you."

Oscaras nodded to his visitors. "You cannot blame them," he said. "There is Marta." He pointed to a pretty, blond woman. "She lost her husband in the first attack. And Joseph—his wife was killed for the food in her pack. They tore Edward's son to pieces like animals."

Captain Picard swallowed. "We're not here to defend these attacks. But Klingons are allies of the Federation. The same laws protect them. What do you know about them? Have you ever left them food or tried to make peace?"

An old man in the crowd laughed. "You are right, Oscaras. Let them go into the forest. After they've lost a few friends, they may listen to us."

"Perhaps we should speak to the prisoner," said Data.

A woman moved near Data and sniffed him. "What are you?" she asked, frowning.

"An android," answered Data, tipping his head. "I was created by—"

"Not now, Data," interrupted the captain. "I believe we should see the captive now."

Oscaras led them to a tiny metal shed. It had no

windows and was more weathered than any other building. The wall near the door looked as if something had tried to break its way out.

"You keep him in there?" asked Beverly Crusher, shocked.

"It's better than he deserves," answered Oscaras. "You'll find the prisoner has been tied. He threw himself against the wall so hard we were afraid he might hurt himself."

As Oscaras reached for the lock, Deanna stepped back. She sensed such feelings of hatred and fear that she felt sick.

It was dark and bad-smelling inside the shack. Picard stepped into the darkness. Doctor Crusher and Deanna followed.

"Let's have some light!" ordered Picard.

Oscaras grabbed a lantern. He turned it on.

Deanna gasped. Against one rusty wall, held by ropes, sat a young Klingon. He was circled by bits of rotting food. He blinked and turned away from the light. Then he pulled his thin knees up to his chest as if he were about to be beaten.

Picard swallowed hard. He tried to smile. "*chay. tlhIngan Hol Dajatlh'a'?*"

The Klingon blinked in surprise. He shook his dark, matted hair from his face. He seemed about to speak. But instead he showed his teeth and hissed.

Beverly Crusher looked angrier than the Klingon. "Let him go at once!" she ordered Oscaras. "This is no way to keep an animal, let alone a humanoid! I need to check him over."

"I would be careful, Doctor," warned Oscaras. "He's bitten several of us already."

Deanna saw that the Klingon was watching them all. His eyes, though reddened and wild, seemed wise. He appeared to be about thirteen Earth years. She was glad they had not brought Worf along. Seeing this, he would have surely punched several of the colonists by now.

"I have an idea," said Picard. "Let us beam him aboard the *Enterprise*. Doctor Crusher can look him over in sickbay. Also, we'll see if Lieutenant Worf can talk to him."

"That's impossible," answered Oscaras. "He is going on trial. Also, we are hoping some of the other creatures will try to get him out. He howls when they begin drumming, so they know he is here."

"Then you refuse to release him to us?" asked Picard slowly.

Deanna could see the captain was planning something.

"I'm afraid I must," answered Oscaras.

The captain turned to the Klingon. "*pich vlghajbe',*" he said.

Again, the boy blinked in surprise. "*Lu',*" the boy grunted.

Picard smiled slightly and left the shed. Beverly Crusher gave the boy a smile and followed the captain out. So did Deanna.

In the daylight again, Picard tapped his communicator. "Six to beam up," he ordered.

Oscaras stepped back as his six visitors disappeared from the spot.

Picard and party stepped quickly off the transporter pads. "Take the controls," Picard ordered Data. "Get him up here quickly."

"I am leaving his ropes there," Data said.

"Number One, phaser on light stun," ordered the captain.

A thin, crouched figure appeared on the platform. The Klingon stared wildly at them. Then he saw that his ropes were gone. He leaped to his feet. He was almost to the door by the time Riker stunned him with a glowing ray. Data rushed to catch the young Klingon as he fell.

"To sickbay," said Beverly, leading the way.

"Well," said Ro Laren with worry in her voice, "it looks like we may have chosen sides."

The red face of Raul Oscaras glared at Captain Picard from the viewscreen.

"How dare you steal our prisoner?"

"I'm sure I could find any number of rules that would let me do so," replied the captain. "Federation policy is quite clear on the treatment of prisoners. I might even find some laws that would allow me to put you under arrest."

Oscaras bowed his head slightly and softened his tone. "All right, Captain. Give us another chance. Return to Selva. You may keep the Klingon as long as you like. Nothing more will be said about it."

"Very well," said Picard. "We will inform you of our plans shortly. Out." The captain turned off his screen.

He pressed another button. "Lieutenant Worf, please come to my ready room."

Already on the bridge, the Klingon entered the ready room quickly.

"You've heard that the captured Klingon is aboard?" asked Picard. "Were you told how he was treated on Selva?"

Worf nodded and growled under his breath.

"Have you talked to anyone on the Klingon High Council about this?" the captain asked.

"Yes, I talked to Kang. As I feared, they do not wish to bring up the loss of the colonies. They want to forget that part of history. There will be no official Klingon help in this matter."

"Then we're on our own." Picard nodded grimly. "Worf, you must make friends with that boy. I can see he remembers some of the Klingon language. He will never trust anyone as he will you. You were right. You will have to go down to the planet and find all of them."

"Yes, Captain," Worf nodded. "I am ready. I have known what it is like to be cut off from my people. I had help in finding them again. I will do the same for the Klingon of Selva."

"I have no doubt," said Picard. "Good luck."

Worf could hear the howls and screams as he hurried toward sickbay. He strode into the room to find a skinny, dirty Klingon slashing out with clawlike hands. The phaser stun had worn off, and the boy would let no one near him.

Worf took a big breath. Then he roared in his loudest, deepest voice, "*yitamchoH!*"

The teenaged Klingon whirled. His mouth dropped open. He was looking at something he had never seen before, an adult Klingon! He grabbed a metal tray and began drumming on it with his long fingernails. It was as if he were trying to drive away a spirit. Then he stopped and whispered in Klingon, "Am I dead?"

Worf laughed. The sound of his laughter made the boy start drumming and howling again.

"Enough," Worf said. "We will not hurt you. I promise. I am Worf," said the security officer, tapping his chest. "Do you have a name?"

The boy stopped the drumming. His eyes were wide. "Turrok," he answered.

"Turrok," said Worf. "Welcome to the *Enterprise*."

Worf spoke in kind, somewhat familiar words. At last the boy stopped the screaming and drumming. Still, he held on to the metal tray as if it could protect him.

"Are you hungry?" Worf asked in Klingon.

Turrok blinked and stared.

"Food?" Worf said.

Turrok nodded. His long hair fell over his eyes.

Beverly Crusher came near with a plate full of fruits and sandwiches. Behind her was Deanna Troi carrying a bundle of clothes. They both smiled warmly at the confused Klingon.

"Eat," Worf told the boy. "It is all for you."

Turrok took a peeled banana in his hand. He sniffed

it. Then he stuffed the whole thing in his mouth. He did the same with a sandwich.

"You are doing well, Worf," whispered Deanna. "I sense his fear is fading. Make friends. That's all you can do. We'll leave you alone now. Call me if you need anything."

Worf nodded. Then he turned back to the boy. Turrok was stuffing food in his mouth as if it would be taken away at any moment. He wiped his chin. "No like them," he said, pointing after Deanna and Beverly. "Kill them."

The big Klingon shook his head. "No. They are my friends."

Turrok touched his ridged forehead as if to say they were different. "Evil!" said the boy, staring after the humanoids.

"But you took their food. Their food is not evil."

"Balak say evil," the boy replied.

"Is Balak your leader, your chief?"

"Chief," nodded Turrok. "I want to go home!"

"Home," nodded Worf. "Turrok, do you remember a home before Balak?"

The boy frowned.

"You are a Klingon," said Worf forcefully. "You come from a proud people. You had a mother and a father. You, Balak, and the others are not alone. We are many."

The boy shook his head. The idea was too much for him. He crouched down and began to howl.

"You have much to learn," Worf said quietly. "All of you do. You must lead me to Balak and the others in your tribe."

Fighting tears, the boy looked around the strange room. "They are not here," he replied

"I know," said Worf. "We will go to them."

"If I take you to Balak," the boy said shyly, "will you teach me to be like you?"

"Yes," Worf answered. "I will teach you to be a Klingon. If you fight, you will fight with honor, not like an animal."

Worf held out the clothing. "You will get along better with humans if you wear clothes," he said.

Turrok smiled at last. "We only go naked," he said, "because it frightens them."

Captain Picard leaned back in his chair. It was time to report to Starfleet. The small colony on Selva was in a tense area near the borders of both Romulan and Klingon space. Starfleet had given Picard the job of "sorting out the problem" there. Now he pressed the panel on his desk. "Picard to Starbase 73. Admiral Bryant, please."

A friendly face appeared on Picard's screen. "Hello, Jean-Luc. So, how are things on Selva? What was all the fuss about?"

Picard told Bryant about their meeting with President Oscaras. He described the beaten Klingon boy they now had in sickbay.

"I had no idea," the admiral said. "What's the matter with those people? Why didn't they report this months ago?"

Picard shook his head. "Perhaps they were afraid we would shut down the colony."

"We still might," replied the admiral. "What are your plans?"

"It's dangerous, but Lieutenant Worf and the prisoner may be able to lead us to the rest of the Klingons. We will try to get them to live in peace. If that fails, we will have to move one of the groups off the planet."

Admiral Bryant nodded. "I'll give you as much time as I can. Good luck, Picard. Bryant out."

Picard touched the panel again. "Picard to Worf. How is our young friend?"

"He has agreed to lead me to the other Klingons," came Worf's answer.

"Good," replied Picard. "I would like to have a meeting in one hour."

"May I bring Turrok?" asked Worf.

"Why not?" answered Picard. "He needs to get used to us. Lieutenant, who would you choose to join you and Turrok in search of the Klingons?"

"A large party might scare them. I believe Data and Counselor Troi would be most useful."

Picard nodded. "We will meet in one hour."

Jean-Luc Picard, Will Riker, Data, Deanna Troi, Geordi La Forge, and Ensign Ro waited in the meeting room. The door slid open. Worf entered with a young Klingon. The boy was dressed in gray pants and jacket. A communications badge gleamed on his chest. Worf pushed him gently into the room.

"Welcome, Turrok," said Picard. "Will you please have a seat?"

The teenager was understanding more and more Klingon, and he wore the universal translator. He nodded and rushed to an empty chair.

Picard smiled at the boy. Then he began the briefing. "Turrok will lead Lieutenant Worf to the rest of the Klingons. Worf believes that Data and Counselor Troi can help him convince the Klingons to make peace. I am worried about the danger." The captain looked at Deanna Troi, as did Will Riker.

The Betazoid smiled. "I'm sure I'll be safe with Data and Worf. If there is any danger, we can beam up to the *Enterprise*."

Geordi La Forge spoke up. "Ensign Ro and I have been studying charts. They have a big problem on Selva a short way offshore. If the underwater plates move any more, there could be a strong earthquake. And it could be soon."

Picard looked serious. "If Ensign Ro has been working with you, Geordi, perhaps we should station her in the settlement. How does that sit with you, Ensign? You can watch things closely."

Ensign Ro leaned forward and replied, "I'd be happy to continue our study. However, I do sense bad feelings toward me down there."

"Ensign," said Picard, "the colonists on Selva can learn from you in more ways than one. Plus, I know you can handle yourself."

Ro nodded. "Thank you, Captain."

Picard slapped the table. "Then that's it. Ro will be stationed at New Reykjavik. Worf, Data, and Troi will go with Turrok to find the Klingons."

It was a cold, gray dawn when five bodies materialized in the village of New Reykjavik. Worf took a step forward. He looked as if he expected to be stoned. Data took tricorder scans while Deanna gazed around the empty square. Turrok played with the zipper of his jacket.

Ro took the pack off her back. "This is as far as I'm going," she told Deanna.

Oscaras and a handful of colonists came out of the plain, metal dining hall. Seeing humans, Turrok moved close to Worf. The colonists stopped in front of the party of two Klingons, two female humanoids, and an android.

"Good morning," said Oscaras, sounding very businesslike. "Are you ready to get started?"

"Our communicators are set to contact the *Enterprise*," said Data. "Perhaps we should have a communicator that could contact you as well."

"Good idea," said Oscaras. He took a communicator from his pocket and gave it to the android. "If you run into trouble, give us a call. I think you are being foolish, but I really don't want to lose any of you."

Turrok was moving toward the gate, trying to pull Worf with him. Deanna and Data followed them.

"We'll keep you informed," Data called back.

There were no friendly goodbyes for Worf, Data, Troi, and Turrok. A guard opened the heavy, metal gate. With an uneasy feeling, Ro watched her friends go. Then she turned to find herself alone with the silent colonists.

"Ensign Ro," Oscaras said at last, "we have a room waiting for you."

"I would like to see the laboratory and earthquake tracking equipment."

Oscaras pointed to a serious, dark-haired woman.

"Doctor Drayton is the head of our science department. You'll be working under her."

"The lab doesn't open until eight o'clock," said Drayton.

"That's very careless," replied Ro. "With all the ground movement on Selva, someone should watch the equipment at all times." She turned to Oscaras. "I'll sleep in the lab. Where is it?"

"Now, just a minute," cried Drayton. "I'm in charge of that lab. I give the orders."

Ro looked her in the eye. "You can be in charge. You can give all the orders you want. But *my* orders are to watch earthquake activity on this planet. You can help me or not, but I won't let you get in my way. Where are the scanners? In that building over there?"

The Bajoran lifted her pack to her shoulder. She strode off toward one of the largest buildings. Doctor Drayton moved to stop her, but Oscaras grabbed the woman's arm. Ro could hear him.

"Let her go," whispered the president. "If this is the price we have to pay for their help, so be it." Then he turned to another man. "Calvert, I want her watched both inside and outside the lab."

"Yes, sir," the man answered. "It won't be hard to keep track of *her*."

Ensign Ro rubbed her eyes. She had been watching the lab machines for several hours. She'd carefully charted the underwater volcanoes. There was one real trouble spot where fiery rock seemed ready to break through the thin crust of the planet. If there were a major earthquake, would that crust hold together? Or would it split like an eggshell?

The lab building also housed the replicator, radio room, and sickbay. Ro could feel uneasy eyes on her all morning as workers passed the lab. Those eyes reminded her that she was, as Guinan had told her, the Other.

There was, however, one set of friendly eyes. They belonged to a freckle-faced, red-haired girl of about twelve. She was carefully checking some plants growing under lights in a corner of the lab. When Ro looked at the corner, the girl smiled. It was the first smile a colonist had given the Bajoran.

At noon the workers rose and left the lab. They were going to lunch, Ro guessed. But the freckle-faced girl headed her way. "Hi. I'm Myra Calvert," she said.

"Call me Ro," said the Bajoran with a smile.

"They're not very nice to you, are they?" asked Myra. "Is it because you have those bumps on your head? What are you?"

"I'm Bajoran," said Ro. "You've probably never heard of my race."

"Of course I have," replied Myra. "You were driven away from your homes by the Cardassians. Now you don't really have a home planet."

Ro smiled, surprised. "That's right. You're very well informed."

Myra shrugged. "Everybody says I'm a genius. The truth is, I just remember what I read. But I'm like you—nobody quite trusts me."

Ro nodded with understanding. "That's their loss. What are you working on?"

"I study plants," said Myra. "Why did they send you down here? To watch for earthquakes?"

Ro nodded. "I hope we're wrong to be worried. But there's a trouble spot out there in the ocean."

Myra moved closer. "They don't like to hear bad news around here," she said. "For months I've been trying to tell them my idea, but they won't listen to me. I'm just a kid."

"What is it?" asked Ro. "I'll listen."

The girl was about to answer when a tall, blond man entered the lab. "Myra!" he called.

"My dad," whispered the girl. "He's head of security." She called back. "I'm over here, talking to Ro. Can Ro come to lunch with us?"

The man cleared his throat. It seemed he couldn't think of a reason to say no. "All right, but we'll have to be quick. I need to stay by the radio. That team from the *Enterprise* could meet up with those Klingons at any time."

"I don't want to be gone long, either," said the slim Bajoran. She rose from her seat and held out her hand. "I'm Ensign Ro."

"Gregg Calvert." The man nodded uncomfortably. "I see you've met Myra. She can talk your ear off."

"Dad!" the girl cried. Then, as if to get back at him, she said to Ro, "Did I tell you my mom died a long time ago? He's a single parent."

"Myra!" growled Calvert. He smiled at his visitor. "You'll know everything about us in the next ten minutes if Myra has her way."

"I would like that," said Ro.

Just outside the dull walls of the fort, the planet Selva became a different place. As big as Worf was, he felt like a flea on a hairy dog. Black trees stretched as far as the eye could see.

Turrok led Worf, Deanna, and Data between the tree trunks. They were not the only life in the dark woods. In the green leaves overhead, animals were moving—chattering, clicking, grunting. The tree trunks themselves were crawling with insects.

At one point Turrok paused. He peeled back a piece of bark and pulled out a bug. It was as large as a man's thumb. The boy held the crawling creature out to Worf. "Eat?"

The adult Klingon shook his head. The youth popped the bug into his mouth. Then he headed on, chewing happily.

After they had gone some distance, Turrok stopped. He seemed to be searching the forest floor for something. He ran to a fallen log.

"Mister Chuck," he said politely to the log, "please give me your home for my far voice." He tapped gently on the log. A black, ratlike creature crawled out. It showed the visitors some very sharp fangs. Then it crawled into the forest.

Now Turrok began to pound on his log. Tat-tat-tat, pause. The forest became strangely quiet. The boy repeated his signal.

Finally Worf heard two taps and a pause from faraway. Turrok answered with a longer set of beats and pauses. Worf looked at Data. He knew the android was storing the patterns and would be able to repeat them perfectly.

Turrok did not look happy. "Tribe is glad I am alive," he said. "But not happy you with me. Before day is over, you may die, or you may kill."

They continued walking. Data watched his tricorder. Soon he announced, "Several large life forms moving our way."

"Phasers on light stun," Worf ordered.

Deanna, who seldom held a phaser, drew hers. When Turrok saw the weapons, he ran into the trees and disappeared.

"How will we find them now?" asked Deanna.

"I believe they will find us," answered Data.

It was only a matter of seconds before dark shapes circled the travelers. The drumming stopped.

Worf tapped his communicator badge. "Worf to *Enterprise*," he breathed. "Stand by to beam three on my command."

"Locked on," replied a voice. "Standing by."

"I count eleven," said Data. "Now thirteen."

"*NuqueH*!" barked Worf. He put his weapon in his jacket pocket and held up empty hands. "We mean no harm!" he said in Klingon.

Deanna put her phaser away. Data did the same.

The Klingons, dressed in black animal skins, moved closer. One reached out to touch Data. The android let himself be pawed. A thin, teenaged girl touched the bony ridges on Worf's head. Then she tapped her own forehead, smiling.

Suddenly the youths backed away as if frightened. Worf turned to see a boy who was at least a head taller than the others. He was pushing Turrok roughly toward the gathering. He was probably sixteen, the oldest of the band. There could be little doubt that this was Balak.

In crude Klingon, the sixteen-year-old growled angrily, "Turrok returns, but he has been with the flat-heads. Tonight he will take the Test of Evil!"

Worf stepped toward Balak. "Turrok has been brave," he said. "He should be treated as a hero."

Balak frowned. "Only the dead are heroes. Who are you? A pet of these flat-heads?"

Worf kept his temper. "This is Data and Deanna Troi," he said. "I am Worf. We have come from a great ship in the sky."

"We have no need of you," Balak replied. "Go away. Be thankful you live."

"You do need us," Worf said. "You were not born in these woods. You come from an empire of people like yourselves and me. We are Klingons."

Data spoke up in crisp Klingon. "You are incorrect to make war on humans, or flat-heads as you call them. Klingons and humans are at peace."

Balak turned on Data. "Don't tell me what to do!" Like a tiger, he jumped on the android and tried to choke him. Data easily pulled his hands away.

"Knives! Knives!" screamed Balak.

Before Worf could draw his phaser, two youths

grabbed Deanna. They held knives to her throat.

Worf slapped his communicator badge and shouted, "Three to beam up. Energize!"

As the Klingons pressed their knives into Deanna's neck, she faded into lights. Another boy slashed at Worf's back, but struck only air.

Worf, Deanna, and Data appeared on a transformer pad aboard the *Enterprise*. Deanna touched her throat. It was bleeding from a slight cut. She swallowed and began to breath again.

Both Worf and Data rushed to her side.

"I know I'm bleeding," she said. "I don't think it's bad. It will heal by itself."

Worf shook his head. "I have failed," he said. "They would not listen."

Data tipped his head. "I believe this is not our easiest mission. We must go back. The sooner the better."

"You do not have to go," Worf told the Betazoid. "It's too dangerous."

"Nonsense," smiled Deanna. "After our disappearing act, I'd like to see their faces."

Worf turned to the surprised transporter operator. "Return us," he ordered. "And make sure the transporter controls are watched at all times."

Worf, Data, and Deanna stepped back on the pads. All three drew their phasers.

"Energize," ordered Worf.

Again, the three officers appeared on the planet with their phasers ready to fire. But they stood alone in the forest of Selva.

Data, Worf, and Deanna pushed through the forest. They followed Data's tricorder readings, hoping to catch up with the Klingon band.

They stopped only when a voice sounded on their communicators. "Picard to away team."

"Worf here," answered the Klingon.

Picard had learned of their visit to the transporter room. He was worried. Deanna told him that she was fine. Data brought the captain up-to-date on their search for the Klingons.

"We talked briefly," said the android. "Then they attacked us."

"The problem is their leader," said Deanna. "I think he sees us as a threat to his power."

"We must keep up the chase," Data insisted. "We are in no danger at present."

"Keep us informed," ordered the captain. "Picard out."

Darkness was falling on the forest. The drums began to beat. Data tipped his head. Then he changed direction.

They moved quickly now. It was getting darker, and the drums were getting louder. There was something up ahead. Just in front of them, the trees ended and a hill began. It wasn't an ordinary hill. It was a steep mound of dirt with young trees growing on it.

"This is unusual," said Data. He marched up the side of the mound. "This is the first rise we have seen. It is also perfectly oval. I would say someone built it."

"Built a pile of dirt?" asked Worf.

"Such things are not unknown," answered Data. "On Earth, early humans built mounds. They served as a place to bury the dead." He looked around. "If this were a natural hill, the trees would be as tall as those in the forest. These clearly are not."

"Sshh," warned Worf. "Listen."

The drumming was louder.

"Let us get back to the trees," said Worf.

Data and Deanna followed him. They hid at the edge of the darkening forest.

In the dim light, they watched a grim parade come out of the trees. There were two drummers at the lead. They were followed by six marchers who carried a wooden cage over their heads. Then came two more, holding a rope. The rope was tied to the neck of a figure who walked alone. His hands were tied behind his back. Ten or so youngsters followed him. They were led by the tallest figure, who banged on a piece of metal with a knife.

The parade climbed to the top of the mound. The figures were dark against the red sky. The drummers stopped drumming. The marchers set down the cage. Deanna knew that the prisoner was Turrok. She knew that the tall one with the knife was Balak.

Balak raised the knife over his head. "Knife-god," he chanted in Klingon, "Giver of Death and Truth, tell us if Turrok is filled with evil. Taste his blood. If he is good, let him live. If he is evil, *kill him!*"

The drummers began beating their drums wildly. The young Klingons clapped their hands. Balak cut the ropes from Turrok's neck and hands. He pushed him inside the cage. Then the big Klingon raised the knife as if he were going to stab the boy. Deanna gasped. But Balak stuck the knife into the side of the cage. There its deadly blade stuck fast, pointing toward the shivering Turrok.

Balak grabbed the cage. He turned it over on the ground. Then he pushed it toward the Klingon beside him. Each person in turn rolled and spun the cage. The drums beat faster. The cage turned over and over again with Turrok falling against the knife countless times.

Worf growled and jumped to his feet. Data pulled him back. "He may already be dead," whispered the android. "We cannot break into their ceremony."

Worf nodded and looked away.

Finally Balak stopped the cage with his powerful arms. The drumming ended. Hands reached forward to open the cage. They pulled the bloody body out. Deanna held her breath.

A girl shouted, "He lives! He lives!"

There were cheers. Turrok was lifted high into the air like a hero. He seemed, however, to have little strength left. As the drums beat again, laughing youths carried the boy down the mound and into the forest.

Now Balak stood alone on the hill. He pulled his knife from the cage and wiped it on his chest. Suddenly he stopped and sniffed the air. Was it her imagination, Deanna wondered, or did he look right in their direction? Then the big Klingon grabbed the cage and ran after his friends.

"Balak will have to be dealt with," Data said.

"Yes," growled Worf angrily. "He will have to be dealt with."

"How?" whispered Deanna. "How will we ever get them to lay down their weapons and live in peace?"

"To gain their respect," said Data, "one of us could take the Test of Evil. This mound is a part of their religion. We should set up camp and wait for them here." He rose to his feet and marched to the top of the hill.

Deanna looked at Worf. "I haven't got any better ideas. Have you?"

"Yes," replied Worf. "But they all involve smashing Balak in the mouth." He grabbed his pack and climbed after the android. The Betazoid followed.

Ensign Ro enjoyed her lunch with Myra Calvert and her father, Gregg. Gregg Calvert said little during the meal, but it was clear that he loved his daughter. Ro said even less. She was happy to listen to Myra tell how they came to the colony.

Her mother and father, Myra explained, had met aboard a science ship. Her mother had the dangerous job of charting asteroids from a shuttlecraft. Just two years after Myra was born, her mother was killed in a shuttle accident.

Gregg turned his back on space travel. He returned with his daughter to Earth. There he met Raul Oscaras. Oscaras promised him a good life in a new colony. Gregg took the job of security chief. That job had turned into a bad dream, he admitted to Ro. He had been wounded in a Klingon attack. If it hadn't been for a fine sickbay, he told the Bajoran, Myra would be alone.

Ro could tell that Gregg wanted to take an army into the forest and wipe out the Klingons. She found it hard to blame him. After only half a day in New Reykjavik, she could understand why the colonists were tense.

Ro spent the afternoon setting up an alarm. It would wake her if there were a big jump in the equipment readings. She also set two scanners to watch the ocean floor. They recorded every grain of sand that moved. Without staying awake twenty-four hours, it was the best she could do. She would sleep right beside her equipment on a cot.

Everyone else left the lab for the night. By evening, the room was quiet except for the hum of the machines.

Then the metal door opened with a whoosh. Ro turned to see the head of the lab, Doctor Louise Drayton. The small, dark-haired woman strode toward her. She looked as if she wanted to chew her head off and spit out the bumps.

Drayton pointed to the cot. "What's the meaning of this?" she snapped.

"It's to sleep on," answered Ro.

"Listen," the woman frowned, "I have a lab to run. Spirits are low enough, so I'm going to try to get along with you. We just need to work out some rules."

"What kind of rules?" asked Ro.

Drayton took a deep breath. She seemed to be trying to calm herself. "If you don't openly go against me, I'll try to bend a few rules to suit you. I only ask that you come to me before you take any action on your own."

Ro nodded. "Very well. I'll check with you, but I won't let you get in the way of my job."

Drayton nodded back. "And I won't let you get in the way of mine," she replied. "Good night."

Ensign Ro watched the dark-haired woman until the door clanged shut behind her.

No one else came to the lab that night. At last Ro couldn't keep her eyes open any longer. She stretched out on her cot.

The night was quiet, except for periods of drumming that sounded far away. In spite of her worries and the bright laboratory lights, the Bajoran fell asleep.

She had no idea what time it was when she awoke. For a moment, she did not remember where she was. But Ro certainly knew *what* had awakened her. She could feel something crawling on her chest under her shirt. She did what anybody would do. She slapped at her chest to brush it off. There was a sharp, stinging pain that took her breath away. She gasped. Now she knew she was in some kind of trouble. She sat up in her cot.

A deep, throbbing pain stabbed her chest. Alarmed, she ripped at her top. Then she screamed as something crawled down her stomach. It bit her again.

Leaping to her feet, she shook her shirt. A bright green creature tumbled to the floor. It looked like a stick with legs. Usually Ro would never take the life of any living thing. But she didn't want the giant insect to get away before she could find out what it was. She stamped on it with her boot, grinding it into the floor.

Ro could hear footsteps on the floor above her. She knew that her scream had been loud enough to get attention. Suddenly her thumping heart, throbbing chest pains, and the footsteps overhead all turned into one giant drumbeat. It pounded in her head. The Bajoran staggered around the lab. Her head felt as if it might explode. Lights flashed before her eyes. She felt as though the crushed insect had wormed its way into her brain. She didn't even know that she was screaming.

Strange, far-off voices shouted at her. Arms grabbed her. "Sickbay," she heard someone yell. Pain and lights exploded in her head and rushed down her body. She felt like she was on fire.

She knew she was dying.

Ro saw lights in the distance. She was running, running, but getting nowhere. They were chasing her—giant skull-faced Cardassians! She was a little girl again, running for her life.

She saw her father. He was beaten, bleeding. The Cardassians struck him down. The little girl could hear the blows. Then everything faded.

When Ro awoke from her nightmare, arms were holding her down. No, not arms, straps. She was tied to an examination table in a sickbay.

"Ro!" a small voice called. "You're awake!" Smiling down at her was the worried face of Myra Calvert.

"I'm awake," sighed the Bajoran, "but I seem to be strapped down. What happened?"

"You were going crazy," said Myra. "They had to strap you down or you would have hurt yourself. You're in our sickbay. You're lucky," the girl said. "You were bitten twice. Nobody's lived after *two* bites from a pit mantis." Myra frowned. "It's strange. We take care to keep those things out. I'll have to see if any of the bugs in the lab cages escaped."

A young man in a doctor's coat appeared behind Myra. He leaned over Ro. "You need rest," said the settlement doctor as he untied the straps. "You'll feel weak for at least twenty-four hours. Now, I must report to Doctor Drayton."

"Doctor Drayton?" asked Ro. "What has she got to do with this?"

"She has been studying the planet's insect life," replied the doctor. "She keeps a record of all serious bug bites. In fact, the pit mantis is a special project of hers."

Ro slumped back on the bed. Suddenly she felt a little sicker.

At daybreak, Worf climbed out of his sleeping bag. The mound rose above the morning fog like an island. Data sat calmly on the slope, watching the forest. Deanna Troi still slept, curled into a ball.

"They are out there," Worf said to Data.

"Yes," said Data. "There are eight of them. They have been watching us."

Worf looked into the trees. Then he cleared his throat and bellowed, "We want to be your friends! We will remain here until you accept us as friends, as Turrok did."

Some chattering and muttering sounds came from the forest. A Klingon girl stepped out of the trees. She stood at the bottom of the slope.

"Is Turrok well?" Worf asked the girl.

"He lives!" she called. "The knife-god said Turrok not evil. Maybe you are not evil either, but you come with flat-heads."

"I am like you," Worf answered. "We are brothers and sisters. Everywhere but here we live in peace with humans."

Deanna Troi was wide-awake now. She moved to

Worf's side. "You are doing very well," she whispered. "I think we can reason with her."

"Until she pulls out her knife," muttered Worf. He called out, "Can we sit and talk? We have food!"

Deanna and Data began digging out candy bars, biscuits, and packaged food.

Now the girl and three brave boys were headed up the slope. They kept their hands on their knife handles. Their noses twitched at the smell of the unusual food. Balak was not among them.

Data opened a package of cherry cobbler and the Klingons moved closer. Deanna held a communicator badge. "I'd like to put this on the girl," she explained to Worf. "Then she can understand me. Tell her it won't hurt her."

Pointing to his own communicator badge, Worf turned to the girl. He spoke in Klingon. "We would like you to wear this as a sign of friendship. It will let you understand us. It will not hurt you."

Deanna's smile won her over. She let the Betazoid fasten the badge inside her furry shirt. "Inside," said Deanna, "so Balak won't see it."

The girl blinked in surprise. She understood the flathead's language.

Deanna held out a candy bar. "Try this."

The female Klingon edged closer. She grabbed the treat and stuffed it into her mouth. Her three friends grunted as if they wanted to steal it.

"I am Worf," the older Klingon said.

"Wolm," said the girl with a smile. She pointed to her friends. "Pojra, Krell, and Maltak."

The three nodded as they gobbled cherry cobbler.

"If the colonists gave you food like this, would you stop attacking them?" asked Worf.

Wolm stopped eating a moment. "I would," she said carefully. "But we have laws—not allow us."

Worf growled. "You have Balak, you mean."

"He is the voice of the laws," she said.

"Where is Balak now?" asked Deanna.

"Seeing the goddess," Wolm answered.

"The goddess?" asked the Betazoid. "Can you tell me more about her?"

Wolm had other things on her mind. She pointed to the empty cobbler wrapper. "More of that!"

Worf spotted eight more skinny Klingons coming out of the woods. He could see them licking their lips. He tapped his badge. "Worf to *Enterprise*."

"Riker here," came the worried voice. "Are you in danger?"

"Only of running out of food," answered Worf. "Can you beam down fifteen full-course meals? Have you ever heard the saying, The way to a Klingon's heart is through his stomach? Well, it's true."

"Your food is on the way," the commander laughed. "On a more serious note, look out for any thin green insects. There's a type of mantis down there that can kill. One of them nearly killed Ensign Ro last night. She seems to be safe now."

"Thank you," replied Worf. "Away team out."

Fifteen steaming plates appeared on the ground. Surprise did not keep the youths from attacking the food.

As the Klingons fought over the food, Worf shook his head. "I hate to see them acting like savages," he said.

"They know no other way," said Deanna gently. "They've only lived this strange life. Every day has been a struggle just to stay alive. I think you should be proud of them."

The morning was suddenly broken by the pounding of a drum. Wolm, Pojra, Krell, Maltak, and the others listened breathlessly. Then, carrying as much food as they could, they began to hurry away.

"We must go," Wolm said. "Balak is back."

"Wolm!" called Data after her. "Tell Balak that I wish to take the Test of Evil to prove my honesty."

She blinked in surprise. "I tell him," she promised. She ran down the hill and was gone.

Data thought. "There is something they like in addition to food." He tapped his badge. "Data to *Enterprise*. I need twenty rhythm instruments. Send snare drums, kettledrums, gongs, and rattles."

Deanna Troi shook her head. "I'm not so sure the settlers are going to like this."

Myra Calvert pushed the juice closer to Ro. "The doctor said you should drink," she reminded her.

But Ro's mind was not on juice. "Let's talk about something else," she said. "Tell me about Doctor Drayton. I only met her once."

"Louise Drayton," Myra began, sounding like a computer. "Born in Canada fifty-three years ago—"

"Can I come in?" a voice broke in from the door of the sickbay.

"Daddy!" cried Myra.

Ro waved weakly to him, "Please do."

As the handsome, blond man neared the bed, Myra said proudly, "My dad saved you last night!"

"Thank you," said Ro.

"And look at those scratches you left on him!" said Myra.

Ro frowned. "Did I do that? I'm sorry."

Gregg smiled. "I haven't been scratched by a woman in a long time."

Ro smiled back, looking into his eyes.

"I just wanted to see how you were doing," Gregg said, blushing. "I hope you'll be well enough to have dinner with Myra and me."

Ro nodded. "Thanks for everything."

As the tall blond man strode out of sickbay, Myra beamed. "I think he likes you."

Ro didn't know what to say, so she changed the subject. "Yesterday," she began, "you started to tell me about an idea of yours. You said it was bad news and no one wanted to hear it."

"Oh, yeah!" exclaimed Myra. "I first thought of this when a big tree was knocked down by lightning. I counted the rings on the trunk. There were only ninety of them. It was the biggest tree on this part of the planet, and it was only ninety years old. Ever since then, I've been trying to find something older than ninety years. I haven't found it yet! My idea is that ninety years ago something—or someone—wiped out everything on Selva. But no one wants to listen to me."

Ro sat up straight. "But if you're right, and that same thing happens again—"

"Yep," said the girl. "This whole colony—the Klingons, too—we're history."

"There aren't any mountains we can study, are there?" asked Ro.

"Nope," answered the girl. "This whole area is like a clean slate. That's what's scary."

"Tomorrow," said Ro, "I want to take a trip to the ocean."

The girl laughed. "Nobody can travel through the forest."

"We've got the *Enterprise*," Ro reminded her. "We don't have to walk there."

"I shall use the kettledrum," said Data. He chose a large drum from the pile of instruments in front of him. He began to beat a rhythm.

Worf watched the forest and listened. He held up his hand, and Data stopped beating. They heard a faraway drummer answer.

"Balak is coming," said the android.

They waited, peering at the trees. At last the drummers came out of the forest. They were followed by more Klingons. They carried the cage that was used for the Test of Evil. There was no prisoner this time, only Turrok. Two boys half-carried him as he tried to walk. Then came Balak and the rest of the tribe. The leader did not look pleased as he banged his knife on his piece of metal.

Deanna held out some of the gifts.

Balak frowned angrily. "You give us food, then toys. Do you think we are children?"

"No," said Worf. "We want to be friends."

"We have laws!" growled the teenager. "You must prove yourselves worthy."

"We will," answered Data. "I will take the Test of Evil.

"Each of you must take a test," Balak declared. He pointed to Deanna. "You will take the Test of Finding." Then he glared at Worf. "Your test will be *me*."

"I will not fight you to the death," said Worf. "We came to make friends, not to kill."

Balak held up his hands.

Now Worf smiled. "Bare hands, yes."

Balak turned to Data. "You first."

"If we pass these tests," said Worf, "will you accept us? Will you let us live among you?"

"Yes!" cried Wolm. "That is fair."

"All right," Balak grumbled. "Make a circle!"

The drummers began a slow beat. Data stepped calmly into the big cage. The Klingons were surprised by his bravery.

Balak held the knife over his head. "Knife-god," he snarled, "Giver of Death and Truth, if this flat-head is evil, kill him!"

Balak stuck the knife between the bars. The blade pointed right at the android's middle. Then he grabbed the cage and turned it over several times. Data stumbled around inside.

Then, unlike the night before, Balak rolled the cage right down the side of the mound. There were gasps from the Klingons as it clattered to the bottom and bounced against the trees.

They gasped even more loudly when Data stepped out of the cage. His uniform was cut to pieces, but the android was none the worse for wear. He picked up the cage and carried it up the mound.

"*Qapla'*!" shouted Wolm. Others joined her cheer. Turrok laughed out loud.

Balak shook with rage. "How did you—? Never mind." He turned to Deanna. "You are next—the Test of Finding."

"I will explain it," said Wolm, stepping forward. "I can speak with Deanna."

Balak nodded.

"Deanna," said the young female, "this is a test for women. We cannot be stronger than men, but we are smarter. You must run into the woods and hide. If the boys cannot find you, then you pass the Test of Finding."

"Hide-and-seek," said Troi. "Very well. How much time do I have?"

"One thousand drumbeats."

The boys stood ready to run. The lead drummer banged his drum. By the time the fifth beat sounded, Deanna had dashed into the trees.

She ran until she was out of sight. Then she pressed her communicator badge.

"Troi to transporter room. Beam me up."

As crashing footsteps sounded in the woods, Counselor Troi transported up. She was in a hiding place where the young Klingons would never look.

Deanna chatted with the transporter operator aboard the *Enterprise* while the Klingons combed the woods. After some time passed, she said goodbye and returned to the planet. The woods were quiet now. The drums had stopped. Deanna walked out of the forest and up the mound. She saw angry looks on the faces of Balak and some of the other boys. Wolm and the girls were smiling.

"She wins the Test of Finding!" declared Wolm.

Worf turned to Balak. He said in Klingon, "It is time for my test."

The young Klingon crouched low. He began to circle Worf. The drummers started a beat. Deanna held her breath. Worf was a bit taller, but both Klingons were strong and heavy.

They growled at each other. Deanna wondered if the lack of weapons really meant that both would come out alive.

Balak lunged first. He tried to throw Worf to the ground. Worf struck Balak's arms and face, but the younger Klingon drove forward. Worf fell back against a young tree. Then he was up again, and they locked arms, grunting like bulls.

Worf drew first blood with a hard chop to Balak's nose. Balak countered with a kick to Worf's mouth that put him down.

Deanna looked at Data. His hand was already over his communicator badge.

But Worf rolled forward. He stuck his head into Balak's middle, tossing him over his head. Together they tumbled down the hill. Both were bleeding and panting.

At the bottom of the mound, they got on their feet again. Balak tried to wrestle Worf to the ground. Worf called on a final burst of strength. He drove Balak's head back into a low-hanging branch. The crack of the branch was louder than the drums. Balak stumbled forward, his eyes glassy. He fell and lay still. The drums stopped.

Worf staggered, too. Then he fell to his knees. Data and Deanna rushed to his side.

"Do not—call—the *Enterprise*," gasped Worf. "I will live."

Wolm, Turrok, and a few others moved closer.

"You beat him," Turrok whispered, as if such a thing were impossible.

"He is a fine fighter," panted Worf.

Up on the mound, some of the Klingons knew what to do. They picked up the rattles, gongs, and drums. They began making a racket loud enough to wake the dead. It did, in fact, wake Balak. He rolled over, holding his bloody head.

He looked at Worf and laughed, "Good fight!"

Worf nodded. A painful smile stretched across his lumpy face. "Very good," he agreed.

When the two big Klingons laughed, everyone laughed. Then the rest of the Klingons picked up the new instruments and banged them for hours.

The young Klingons played atop the mound for at least two hours. They tried out all the gongs, drums, and rattles. As the others danced, Balak tried to fix the cage, which was broken during Data's Test of Evil.

The tribe was made up of twenty-one Klingons. There were fourteen boys and seven girls. The oldest appeared to be Balak. The youngest was Turrok. Forty-eight children had set out on the refugee ship. More than half of them had not lived through the crash landing or this rugged life.

Balak had finished tying the cage back together. He stood and shouted, "We go to hutch!"

The Klingons quickly got in a line. They marched down the mound. Deanna, Worf, and Data followed them into the forest.

After following a faint trail, Balak came to a stop. He lifted what looked like a mat woven from grass, leaves, and twigs. It had been hiding a dark tunnel that went deep into the ground. Balak quickly dropped to all fours. He crawled in. The others looked at Worf. It was clear that they wanted him to follow. Data stepped to the front.

"Lieutenant," he said, "since I can see much better in the darkness, would you and Counselor Troi follow me?"

"Certainly," said Worf. He seemed happy to let the android lead the way into the hole.

When Deanna's turn came, she held her breath. Loose dirt fell onto her face. Finally, she closed her eyes. There was no reason to keep them open. It was pitch-dark. She moved along the mud in a sea of blackness.

At last she came to a place where she could stand. She heard a stick gently tapping on the tunnel roof. A ray of gray light swirled down from a shaft. It wasn't much, but any light was welcome.

Deanna saw Worf looking around the burrow. He found a place where he could stand straight up.

"Is this your only hutch?" Worf asked.

"No," said Balak. "We keep many hidden from the flat-heads."

Worf pulled a tube from his pocket. "Have you ever seen a flashlight?" he asked. He turned it on.

"Light indoors—I remember it!" declared Balak. "When I was little, there was a place called nursery. We had light. Long time ago. Hard to remember." He shook his head sadly. Right now, thought Deanna, he looks like a little boy.

A voice broke into her thoughts. "Picard to away team."

Data answered, "Away team here. The mission is going well. We have been accepted by Balak, leader of the Klingons. We are with him now in an underground shelter. You may speak freely. Only Turrok and a female named Wolm are wearing communicator badges. Balak will not be able to understand us."

"I wanted you to know that Ensign Ro has asked to make a trip to the ocean. We are transporting a small party to the seashore tomorrow. It probably would be best if the Klingons did not meet them there."

"Understood," answered Data. "We will stay here and continue to win their trust."

"Excellent," said Picard. "Out."

The mud hole was lighter now, but it was still very cold and damp. Deanna shivered. "I would like to sleep outside," she said.

"I will keep you company," said Data. He turned to Balak and spoke in Klingon. "Counselor Troi and I are going outside. Perhaps Lieutenant Worf would like to stay inside with you."

Deanna started back up the tunnel. Data followed her.

"Use the roots to pull yourself up!" Balak called after them.

Balak tapped Worf's shoulder. "Storm coming. You better off here." He looked up the light shaft to study the sliver of sky. "Yes, a storm," he smiled. "Good night to see goddess."

"Goddess?" asked Worf. "You spoke of her before."

"Goddess for me now," Balak said. "You later."

Several Klingons had gathered in the burrow now. Worf sat with them by the light of his flashlight. He answered questions about the great Klingon empire. Some of them remembered a place that was different from the forest. This place sounded like the cities Worf described.

As the night wore on, the burrow became quiet. Even Worf began to feel quite comfortable. Turrok cuddled into his chest. Wolm cuddled into his back. He found himself drifting off to sleep.

Above ground, Deanna slept quite comfortably. The bed of leaves was soft, and she was sheltered by the branches of a large tree. Data stood as still as one of the silent tree trunks. He knew that there were Klingon guards in the trees. They watched the forest, especially in the direction of the village. Data's attention was on the entrance to the hutch.

At last the trapdoor moved. A large figure climbed out. Data knew that it was Balak. The big Klingon made some clicking noises. The guards in the branches clicked back. Then he walked into the forest. Data moved silently after him.

Balak skipped along in the dark woods like a boy heading home from school. Once he paused to sniff the air, then he turned quickly. But Data stopped in time and pretended to be a tree trunk.

The android followed until Balak stopped and made a cawing sound. Both he and Data stood still, waiting. Finally a voice floated on the night wind. It called in Klingon, "Come! Come, my follower! Come to me!"

Data knew the sound for what it was. It was a female voice made louder by a good sound system. But Balak heard it as the haunting voice of a goddess.

A frosty white light bounced between the trees. Balak moved toward it.

"Come forward, Balak!" called the voice.

The youth held his hands out. "I—I have returned, goddess!" he whimpered.

"You have not done what I told you!" the voice thundered. "I told you to *kill* the flat-heads! Now you take them into your hutch!"

Data could make out a female shape standing beside a lantern. She seemed to be swaying back and forth.

"They passed the tests," Balak whimpered. "Test of Evil, of Finding, of Strength. They gave us food and drums—."

"Stop!" blasted the voice. A whoosh of cold air swept past him, and Data quickly saw why. The female was walking toward them holding a glowing whiplike weapon. It was a *displacer*! Some say the displacer was invented by the Romulans, some say the Ferengi. But displacers are against the law in the Federation. They are weapons of torture! Now the whip flicked from side to side in front of the goddess. It hissed like a snake's tongue.

Data wondered how strong a shock the weapon could deliver. He was so interested in the displacer that he almost forgot about Balak and the goddess. He forced his attention back to them. The frightened Klingon was creeping forward.

"I'm sorry!" he sobbed. "Forgive me!"

"Yes," the goddess cried. She cracked the displacer in front of the Klingon. He fell back as if punched by a fist. She gave the whip a flick and sent him to the ground. The displacer wrapped itself around Balak's legs. Balak yelped in pain.

"You will kill them," the woman insisted, "or I will kill

you." The goddess circled his neck with the glowing whip.

Still as a tree trunk, the android watched as the goddess pulled the young Klingon toward her. She kissed him hard on the mouth. Then she laughed.

Captain Picard sipped his tea before he looked up. Gathered in his quarters were Commander Data, Counselor Troi, and Lieutenant Worf. Data was just finishing his story of the strange meeting in the forest. Picard had been fast asleep when the call had come from Worf. He insisted that Data had a tale that had to be told. It certainly did, thought the captain glumly.

Deanna shook her head. "You say this 'goddess' told him to kill the settlers? Then she kissed him?"

"That is what happened," agreed Data.

"Captain," said Worf, "we must learn more about this 'goddess'."

The captain's lips were tight. "Romulan," he whispered. "Data, you said the weapon was Romulan?"

The android answered, "Possibly Romulan. Others have linked the displacer to the Ferengi secret police."

"That's enough to make me worry," said Picard. "Officially, the Romulans left this area. But did they really leave? This is supposed to be a neutral zone between the Romulans and the Klingons. It is free space, or so the Federation was led to believe. But what if the Romulans want to claim it? They have been known to use hidden bases for spies."

Worf rose. "Captain," he began, "the Klingons must

break free of this ‘goddess’. To lessen the danger, I shall stay on Selva alone.”

“Lieutenant, you need help. What if you were overpowered in your sleep?” asked Picard. “In fact, I will be beaming to Selva. Ensign Ro wants to make a trip to the ocean, and I’ve decided to join her. At oh-nine hundred I will lead a party of colonists to the seashore. We will use the transporter, of course. I’ll let Ro know what is happening. Please think about your own safety first in everything you do. Dismissed.”

The door to the transporter room slid open. Deanna, Worf, and Data strode to the platform.

“This goddess business is maddening,” growled Worf. “Who would push them into attacking the settlers?”

“Unknown,” answered Data, centering himself on the pad. “But it is likely that there is a spy planted among the colonists.”

Worf nodded. “It doesn’t take much to make a Romulan look human,” he muttered. Then he nodded to the transporter operator. “Energize.”

When they appeared in the woods, they were met by silence. They found their equipment piled under the tree where they had left it. Data moved to the entrance of the tunnel. “We could search the hutch, but I believe the Klingons are gone.”

Worf got on his knees by the hole. “Turrok!” he called. “Wolm!” No answer came from within the dark ground. He jumped to his feet. “Balak!” he yelled.

"There is no point in shouting," said Data. "They are nowhere near, or I would pick them up on my sensors."

Worf muttered, "That is all right. We can track Turrok and Wolm by their communicators."

"No, we cannot," said Data. The android bent down. He brushed away some leaves and picked up two communicator badges.

"Now we're back to square one," sighed Deanna. "We have to find them again."

At some distance, a drumbeat sounded. Data tipped his head in that direction. "To the east," he said, "toward the ocean."

Ro stepped out into the cold morning air. She felt wide-awake and ready to go. Glad to be out of sickbay, she walked briskly toward the center of the settlement. In the village square was a map showing people's homes. She checked it and found the Calvert quarters.

A camera turned to watch her as she neared their door. "State your business," said a computer voice.

"Ensign Ro to see Myra and Gregg Calvert."

"Ro!" called Myra's friendly voice.

Once inside, Ro noticed that Myra and Gregg had worked hard to make their apartment seem like home. The walls were cold, gray metal, but unusual plants and family pictures cheered the room.

"How are you feeling?" Gregg asked Ro.

"Terrific!" she exclaimed. "I feel like walking the twenty kilometers to the ocean."

"Not many people would bet that you would get there," Gregg said glumly. Then he put on a smile. "This is a great favor your captain is doing us. There's only so much you can tell about an ocean by looking at sensors. We were just on our way to breakfast," Gregg added. "Care to join us?"

Ro nodded, suddenly very hungry. "Lead on."

They were not at the dining hall table long before they were joined by Louise Drayton. The dark-haired doctor looked as serious as ever.

"Calvert," she said, "I haven't packed yet. How long before we go?"

Ro nearly choked on her pancakes. "Go where?" she asked.

Louise looked at her. "Why, to the ocean, of course," she replied. "Surely you know I will be joining your party. I've been trying to put together a trip to the shore for three months."

Gregg shrugged. "Half an hour," he answered. "Please don't bring too much, Doctor—just a canteen, a tricorder, and some sample jars. We may have to move quickly. Oh, and bring your phaser. Everyone but Myra will be armed."

Some of Ro's excitement faded. She thought about refusing to let Drayton join the party. But she did not want to make a fuss. "Set those phasers to stun," she said.

Gregg Calvert stood. "I'll let you three finish breakfast. I want to make sure the *Enterprise* has the right coordinates."

"You're worried about this trip, aren't you?" asked Ro.

Gregg replied, “I’m just taking my only daughter, our top scientist, and a visiting Starfleet officer into a place filled with savages. Why should I be worried?”

It was almost time to leave. Ensign Ro, Gregg and Myra Calvert, and Doctor Drayton were gathered in the village square. They were waiting to be transported.

A voice boomed across the square. “Be careful! We can’t afford to lose anyone!” Raul Oscaras came striding toward them.

“We will,” sighed Gregg Calvert. He didn’t need to be reminded of the danger.

Oscaras turned to Ensign Ro. “I’m holding you responsible for this party,” he warned. “This trip was your idea. All right, you may leave.”

Ro could not believe that this man thought he was so important. But she said nothing. She was happy to hear a familiar voice sound over her communicator badge.

“Captain Picard to Ensign Ro. How many in your party?”

“Ro here, Captain. There are four, counting myself.”

“I believe I’ll join you,” said Picard. “Are you ready to beam aboard?”

“Yes,” she said quickly.

Their bodies disappeared in swirls of glittering lights.

Ro, Myra and Gregg Calvert, and Doctor Drayton materialized in the transporter room. Captain Picard was there, dressed in a warm jacket.

"Wow!" said Myra Calvert, eyes wide. "Can we look around?"

Captain Picard stepped onto the platform. "Maybe later."

"Can we get to the ocean?" asked Louise Drayton. "I don't want to waste a second."

"Very well," said Picard, centering himself on the pad. He turned to the transporter operator. "You have the coordinates?"

The operator nodded. "Locked in. If you want to come back quickly, just call."

"We shall," answered Picard. "Energize."

Five visitors appeared on a black beach on the planet of Selva. A copper-colored wave splashed on the sand, dumping red foam on Picard's boot. It left a gray trail where the black shoe polish had been.

"What!" exclaimed Picard. He jumped back.

"Oh, yes," said Doctor Drayton. "The sea foam is high in acid. Don't let it get on you."

As they strode down the beach, Captain Picard tried to get used to colors that seemed all wrong. The forest and beach were black. The sea was copper red. The sky was sickly green. The only healthy green was at the tops of the trees. Picard looked at the toe of his boot. It was now bone white.

Picard turned to the other members of the party. Gregg Calvert was watching the forest. His hand was close to his phaser. Ro was wide-eyed, enjoying all of the strange sights. Picard decided it was time to let her in on all that had happened.

He walked to her side. "Ensign," he said quietly, "while you were sleeping off that insect bite, Commander Data saw something very odd. Balak, the leader of the Klingons, went to see a 'goddess' in the woods. She was a real woman, of course, but she was passing herself off as a goddess. You must be on the lookout for this woman. She could be one of the colonists."

Without thinking twice, Ro looked at Doctor Drayton. The doctor was watching her from a distance, a strange smile on her face.

Selva's ocean made Ro think of an endless pool of blood. The Bajoran could imagine the great slabs of earth on the ocean floor, all being forced upward by hot lava. Perhaps Selva would someday become a planet covered by water. The land masses would all be flooded. It could happen.

Ro's thoughts were cut short by a screeching from the forest. She turned to see a skinny Klingon running toward them. Gregg Calvert drew his phaser.

"Hold your fire!" ordered Picard. "There's only one, and he's unarmed."

But Picard spoke to the wrong colonist. Louise Drayton calmly drew her phaser and took aim. Before she could shoot, Ro flung an arm into her face. She grabbed the phaser and pulled it away.

"What are you doing?" screamed Drayton.

"The captain said not to shoot," snapped Ro. She checked the doctor's phaser. It was set to kill. She reset it to light stun.

Louise Drayton glared, then looked away.

The young Klingon fell to the black sand, breathing heavily. Deep cuts covered his thin body. Ro and Picard rushed toward him while the colonists hung back.

The captain knew this boy. "Turrok!" he cried. He knelt and put his arm around Turrok's shoulders.

Ro drew her phaser and stood guard over them. She

looked both at the forest and at the settlers. She was not sure where trouble would come from first.

"You must go," gasped Turrok in Klingon. "Leave now. They are in the forest."

"How many?" asked Picard in Klingon.

"All," breathed Turrok. "Balak says to attack and kill."

"I see more of them, sir," said Ro. "At the edge of the forest."

Picard didn't wait to see them. He tapped his communicator. "Five to beam up." He looked at Turrok. "Make that six."

Picard's last words were drowned out by shouts from the forest. A dozen young Klingons rushed toward them, all carrying knives. Ro, Picard, and Turrok were closer to the mob than the Calverts. The big youth in the lead was upon them in seconds. Ro fired her phaser. The beam spun the big Klingon around. It dropped him to the ground at their feet.

"Energize," Picard shouted.

From the forest, Wolm watched the humans disappear in sparkling lights. The other Klingons stopped and stared at the strange sight. Then Wolm saw Balak lying on the black beach. She touched her cheek. It was black-and-blue where Balak had hit her the night before. She drew her knife.

Wolm dashed between the other Klingons. She bent over Balak's stunned body. Holding her knife in both hands, she drove it into his chest. His blood gushed over the knife and Wolm's hands. The big Klingon gave a gasp and went to sleep forever.

Wolm shook the knife over the fallen leader. "He had to die!" she declared. "He wanted to kill flat-heads and never make peace. That is not way to live! We cannot kill and kill. They have much to offer. We will learn to fly ships, make food out of air, and change into lights."

The circle of Klingons stared at her. One of the taller youths stepped forward. "You will take Test of Truth!" he cried.

Wolm brushed back her dirty hair. "I will take it," she declared. "But you know I am true."

"The goddess will be angry," warned another.

"Let goddess punish me!" snapped Wolm. "I never see goddess. No one sees goddess but Balak."

"What if she never speak to us again?" asked one young Klingon.

Wolm crossed her thin arms and said, "Then we make our own decisions."

Geordi La Forge gave Myra Calvert a quick tour of the *Enterprise*. Meanwhile, Captain Picard, Ensign Ro, Greg Calvert, and Doctor Drayton met in sickbay. Turrok lay on a table while Doctor Crusher cleaned his wounds.

"Captain," said Gregg Calvert, "can you ask him how they knew where we were going to be?"

Picard held up his hand. He wanted to wait until Beverly Crusher was finished before beginning his questions. "Turrok saved our lives by warning us," he said.

"All right, Captain," said Doctor Crusher, standing back. "If you want to question him, do it gently. He's been stabbed and beaten." Crusher looked at Gregg Calvert and Louise Drayton. "Don't say or do anything that would upset him."

"We won't," said Gregg. "I just want to know how they knew."

Picard leaned over the boy. He placed a communicator badge on the bandages that covered his chest. "I want to thank you for saving our lives."

"Balak," whispered the young Klingon. "He was wrong. Worf, Troi, and Data—they enter our hutch. They join us. Wolm and I are happy. Killing was over. Then Balak go to see the goddess." Turrok tried to get up.

"Don't upset yourself," said Picard. "You're safe here. We're all safe."

"Who is Balak?" asked Gregg Calvert.

"Their leader," said Louise Drayton. "Let him go on."

"What happened after Balak saw the goddess?" asked Picard.

"Before he go, we were friends," said Turrok. "When he come back, he want to kill flat-heads. He said he knew where they would be in the morning."

"The goddess told him that?" asked Gregg.

Turrok nodded. "Worf, Troi, and Data were gone. Balak would not listen to us. He drag us out of hutch and hit us. Took badges from me and Wolm. We walk all night to get there—to the water."

"They were tipped off!" exclaimed Gregg.

Picard gently patted the boy's arm. "You got away from them and warned us?" he asked.

Turrok nodded. He was fighting back tears.

"You rest now," Picard told the boy. "Worf, Troi, and Data will find your friends. They will make peace again."

Captain Picard stood in the turbolift with Ensign Ro, Gregg Calvert, and Doctor Drayton. Geordi was meeting them in the transporter room with Myra. The small party would beam back to New Reykjavik.

Gregg Calvert was shaking his head. "Never in my wildest dreams," he muttered, "did I think there was a *spy* among the colonists!"

"How can you be sure it's one of the colonists?" asked Picard.

"Because this 'goddess' knew where we were going to be this morning," snapped Gregg. "She must be a colonist. There is a spy in our midst! It explains how the Klingons always seemed to know where our parties were going to be. At least she didn't give them phasers."

"That would have tipped you off," said Ro. "You would never have found out about this if Worf and our people hadn't won their trust."

Gregg nodded. "We must make friends with as many of the Klingons as we can, however we can."

The turbolift door slid open. Captain Picard led the way. "I wish you were in charge of the settlement instead of Raul Oscaras," he said to Gregg. "Do what you can to stop the violence."

"Daddy!" cried Myra Calvert as the door to the transporter room opened. "We had a great tour."

Geordi La Forge laughed. "This girl knows her stuff. If you ever send this child to Starfleet Academy, let us know. There will be a place for her aboard the *Enterprise*."

Gregg Calvert hugged his daughter. Then he told her seriously, "I've learned some things, too."

"Riker to Picard," came a worried voice.

The captain tapped his badge. "What is it, Number One?"

"Admiral Bryant wishes to speak with you."

Picard frowned. "Put him through."

"Captain Picard," said a voice, "I hate to do this, but I'm going to pull you away from Selva. I have an important job for you. We've just had a breakthrough over in the Aretian solar system. The Aretians are ready to end a war with their neighbors. They have agreed to let us map their system and divide it up. We have to move quickly before they change their minds."

Picard cleared his throat. "This is a rather important time in this mission. Is there another ship that could do the mapping?"

"You're the closest ship," answered Admiral Bryant. "At warp speed, the Aretian system is only six hours away. I've promised them that you'll be there in ten hours."

"Yes, sir," Picard said.

"You can return to Selva as soon as possible," the Admiral added. "I'll leave it up to you whether you want crew members to stay on Selva while you're gone. I know there are two hundred or so people on the planet. But billions of lives are at stake in the Aretian system."

Picard nodded. "We'll be there in ten hours. Picard out."

"So the *Enterprise* is leaving in four hours?" said Louise Drayton. "That just shows how much you care!"

Captain Picard's back stiffened. "You are wrong, Doctor Drayton," he declared. "Our first interest is peace, but the *Enterprise* is a visitor, an outsider. If you and those young Klingons want to kill each other, we can't stop you. You must end the bloodshed yourselves."

"We understand," said Gregg Calvert. He lifted Myra in his arms. "I am only one person. But I swear I'm going to do everything I can to bring peace to my world."

Louise Drayton followed the others onto the transporter platform. She would not meet Ensign Ro's eyes.

The Bajoran was bothered by Drayton's argument with the captain. The woman seemed to enjoy causing trouble. The ensign shook her head as she stepped to the middle of the platform. She was not happy to be leaving the *Enterprise*. She had a feeling that something terrible was about to happen.

Worf heard the drum beating slowly in the forest. Then he heard voices. A parade wound through the trees. First came the drummers. In the center of the line walked the Klingons who held Balak's body over their heads. Behind them marched other members of the tribe. They seemed to be arguing.

"It is Balak," said Data. "He appears to be dead."

Data, Worf, and Deanna Troi walked down the mound. They watched as the youngsters carried Balak's body up the hill. When they had trouble with the heavy load, Worf hurried to help them. He grabbed Balak by the shoulders. With the big Klingon's aid, they carried the dead sixteen-year-old to the top.

"Go now," one of the youths growled at Worf.

Worf turned to Wolm. He saw that the side of her face was black and blue. "Go Worf," she whispered. "All will be well."

Worf nodded. He reached into his pocket and pulled out a handful of communicator badges. He set them on the ground. "These are for you," he said. Wolm smiled briefly.

Then Worf joined Deanna and Data at the bottom of the hill.

"Captain Picard has asked that we return to the *Enterprise*," the android told him. "This would appear to be a good time to leave them alone."

Lieutenant Worf nodded. He tapped his communicator badge. "Three to beam up."

Two minutes later, the three members of the away team stood in Captain Picard's ready room. Will Riker was there, too. He was being briefed on the new mission. Like the others, Deanna listened as Picard told them about their work in the Aretian system. Then she listened to Data tell of the funeral parade for Balak.

"Balak's death is unfortunate. However, it will probably help our chances of making friends with the Klingons," Data said.

Picard sighed. "I still don't feel right about leaving you on Selva while we map the Aretian system."

"Captain," Deanna said, "I believe it would be a mistake for us to leave now. I don't think any of us feel as if we are in danger."

"Thank you, Counselor." Picard frowned. "But I don't trust *either* of the parties down there. The Aretian system is six hours away. Unless you use the colonists' subspace radio, you'll be out of touch with the ship."

Worf replied, "We understand that, Captain. Still, we do not want to leave. We are so close to solving the problem."

The captain slapped the arms of his chair. "Then you'll stay on Selva," he declared.

Deanna smiled at Worf. She found the big Klingon smiling back.

"Ensign Ro should stay, as well," added the captain. "Data, I'm only leaving four crew members on Selva. But they aren't four crew members I care to lose. I'm counting on you to make the safety of the away team your number one concern."

"Understood, Captain."

Ensign Ro sat stiffly in a chair in President Oscaras's office. Gregg Calvert stood beside her.

The president marched through the door and sat down behind his desk. "Okay, Calvert, what's so important?"

The tall, blond man got right to the point. "Today I found out that we have a spy among us," Gregg declared. "Someone has been secretly meeting with the Klingons and giving them information."

Oscaras laughed. "That's crazy! Nobody would dare go out there by himself. What would be the point of it?"

Gregg leaned across the bearded man's desk.

"As to the point of it, I don't know. But the spy is not just taking a walk out there. *She* is pretending to be a goddess. She's using some kind of Romulan whip and meeting with the leader of the Klingons. In fact, she told him to attack us."

"Please!" said the president. "How could she get outside, past the guards? Why would somebody want to see an attack on her own friends and neighbors?"

"I don't know," muttered Gregg. "But just this morning, we were beamed to a place on the beach. We weren't there fifteen minutes before we were attacked.

How did the Klingons know we were there? Don't tell me they were just in the neighborhood!"

Oscaras looked at Ro. "Well, members of the *Enterprise* crew are Klingons. They knew where you were going. That could explain it."

"But the same thing has happened before!" Gregg declared. "Before the *Enterprise* got here."

"Save your breath, Gregg," said Ro. "President Oscaras isn't interested. He wants to keep the hate alive. It's easy to keep power over a frightened community."

Oscaras angrily pointed a finger at Ro. "I don't need to listen to any Bajoran. I asked for help from Starfleet, and all I got was a bunch of nonhumans. What we need are some armed people to hunt down every last one of those Klingons!"

"I don't believe that's the answer anymore," said Gregg softly. "I think we must try making friends with the Klingons. That is what the *Enterprise* is trying to do."

Oscaras glared at Ensign Ro. His face was red. "She turned your head, didn't she? Not a bad-looking woman, even with those things on her head. Well, Calvert, you and Ro are free to do whatever you want. But you are no longer Security Chief!"

Calvert slammed his hands on the president's desk. "This has nothing to do with Ro. I saw with my own eyes. That boy we kept chained up saved our lives this morning."

"You are to stay in your quarters!" ordered Oscaras. He pointed to the door. "Soon we'll be rid of the *Enterprise*. I do make mistakes, and calling Starfleet was one of them. I should have known they were too buddy-buddy with the Klingons to help us. By the time the *Enterprise* returns, this problem is going to be over!"

Gregg Calvert pounded the desk one last time. Then he marched out the door. Ensign Ro stopped in the doorway.

"You're wrong about Gregg and me," she said. "You're wrong about everything."

"Get out!" Raul Oscaras shouted.

By the time Ro got to the street, Gregg had disappeared. Probably, she thought, he's heading for his quarters.

The Bajoran decided to check the lab. Watching earthquake activity on Selva was her main job, she told herself.

As soon as she looked at her lab equipment, Ro knew that something was wrong. Jagged lines were appearing up and down the screen. The underwater plates were shifting. Volcanic activity was up twenty percent. It could be the beginning of an underwater eruption. Ro held her breath. She waited to see if the activity would increase. It didn't. The charts went back to normal. The shaking in the ocean was letting up.

Ro breathed again. She sat down in her chair. No one else knew how close they had come to disaster. Even now, Ro wasn't certain what was in store for Selva.

Turrok sat beside Worf in the big Klingon's quarters aboard the *Enterprise*.

"You must go back to your forest," Worf said. "We must both go back."

Turrok frowned. "No! I won't go! Balak will kill me."

"Balak is dead," said Worf.

"Dead?" asked the boy, shaking his head. "The flat-heads killed him?"

Worf shook his head. "I did not know how he died."

Turrok suddenly smiled. "I think Wolm killed him. She is very brave. She hate him because he only want to kill."

"Transporter room to Worf," came a voice over Worf's badge.

The Klingon tapped it to answer. "Worf here."

"All ashore that's going ashore. The *Enterprise* will be leaving in ten minutes."

Turrok looked unhappy. "I not want to go back."

"You must," said Worf, seriously. "When the history of Selva is written, you will be one of the founders of a great civilization."

"How do I do that?" asked Turrok.

Worf smiled. "Just by making friends."

Worf, Turrok, Deanna, and Data transported to the sacred mound. They brought along plenty of food. Soon nineteen young Klingons were eating as fast as they could.

"Data," said Worf, "I think the time has come. If you agree, I would like us to walk into the village tomorrow. Let the settlers provide the food."

Deanna looked worried. "Balak may be gone, but these Klingons can still be fierce. We don't know the whole story, but it seems that Wolm stabbed Balak to death as he lay wounded."

"Picard to away team," came a voice. "We're leaving now. We'll be six hours away, so the earliest we can return is in twelve hours. If you can, get into the village to report by subspace radio. I don't want to be out of touch for long."

"We will make it to the village," replied Worf.

"Don't expect miracles," said Picard. "Just keep yourselves alive. *Enterprise* out."

Ensign Ro was watching her instruments closely. The voice on her communicator badge surprised her.

"Picard to Ro."

"Ensign Ro here."

"Is everything under control?" he asked.

Ro swallowed. "I don't trust those underwater plates," she answered, "or Raul Oscaras."

"I'm worried, too," Picard said. "The ship is leaving orbit now, but we'll return as soon as possible. It may be as few as fourteen or fifteen hours. Look out for yourself. Use the colonists' radio if you need to."

"Understood, sir," answered Ro.

"Picard out."

Ro sat back in her chair. There didn't seem to be much she could do except watch the sensors and hope that there were no more quakes.

A little voice broke into the Bajoran's worried thoughts. "Ro?"

She turned to see a young girl with very large, red eyes. Ro opened her arms and hugged the child. Myra sobbed.

"They kicked him out of his job," she cried. "My poor dad. I feel awful for him. He's done all he can, and they're stupid!"

"Myra, someone had to break with Oscaras. Your father was the first. There will be others."

Myra nodded. "Thanks," she said, wiping her nose, "but it's hard."

Ro nodded. Then she glanced at her instruments. "Not to change the subject, but there was some shaking out there in the ocean. I just wonder if you have any thoughts about it."

"Well," answered Myra, "I think I know what happened to the forest. It has something to do with what you're doing."

"What do you mean?" asked Ro. Her heart beat faster.

"I mean," said Myra, "what happened ninety years ago wiped out the forest. If you go outside our gate and dig in the ground, you'll find black sand, like we saw on the beach today. I think that ninety years ago a giant tidal wave—a tsunami—rolled across here. It wiped out everything."

"Could that happen again?" asked Ro.

"It will happen again," answered Myra. "In ten thousand years or ten years. Who knows?"

"It could happen anytime," whispered Ro. She

looked at her instruments. "What exactly causes a tsunami?"

"An earthquake or volcanic eruption in the ocean," answered Myra. "It would have to be a big one. The shores can get hit with walls of water."

"Have you told this to any of the others?" asked Ro. "They must be warned."

"They won't believe me," Myra said.

"Myra," Ro said, "you've got to take me to the radio room. I have to call the *Enterprise*."

"Come on." Myra grabbed Ro's arm.

They climbed the metal stairs to the second floor. Ro knew the replicator, sickbay, and radio room were located there. Right away, three brown-suited colonists met them.

A big man stepped in front of Ro. "What do you want?" he demanded.

"To use the radio," she said.

"You need an okay from President Oscaras," the man replied.

"My dad will give her an okay," declared Myra.

"Your dad is not allowed to leave his quarters," growled the man. "Now get out of here, both of you."

Ro reached up to tap her communicator badge. But who was she going to call? The *Enterprise* was light-years away. She put her arm around Myra and steered her out the door.

When the door shut behind them, the girl burst out. "My dad will take care of them!"

For Myra's sake, Ro tried to hide the fear that was

rising inside her. "Why don't we go talk to your dad," she said.

Gregg Calvert was sitting in his room, looking very glum indeed. "Look," Ro said to him. "I have to get to that radio and call the *Enterprise*. We've just had a major earthquake. Your daughter and I believe another one might cause a tidal wave that could swallow the colony. I want to call the captain and tell him to get everyone off this planet."

Gregg Calvert never questioned Ro. He stood. "Okay, let's see what we can do." He turned to his daughter. "I'm sorry, sweetheart, but I want you to stay here. This may get ugly. Don't go to the lab or anywhere. We'll be back as soon as we can." He turned to Ro. "Let's go talk to Oscaras."

They found the president in the replicator room. The replicator was quickly turning out new phaser rifles.

"You're supposed to stay in your quarters," Oscaras said to Gregg Calvert as he and Ensign Ro entered.

"I don't care what you do to me," said Gregg, "but Ro is a Starfleet officer. She wants to use the radio."

"That would be impossible at the moment," said Oscaras. "You see, we're on a security alert."

Ro eyed the piles of phaser rifles. She decided that arguing wouldn't get them very far. "I'll try again tomorrow," she said. She edged toward the door.

"Stop her!" screamed a voice.

They turned to see Doctor Louise Drayton. "Get her

communicator badge," she shrieked, "before she calls the Klingons!"

Ro ducked past Oscaras and ran for the door. There were shouts behind her, but she kept running down the hall. Looking over her shoulder, she saw Gregg trying to hold back Oscaras, Drayton, and some other colonists. Someone hit him with the end of a phaser rifle. He dropped to his knees. Ro darted down the stairs and out of the building.

"Stop," shouted Oscaras. He was in the street now, holding a rifle. "Let's talk about this!"

Louise Drayton came up behind him and grabbed his weapon. "What are you waiting for?" she screamed. She lifted the rifle and took aim.

"No!" cried Ro. She held up her hands. The blue beam ripped through her body until it reached her brain. There it exploded in a white-hot flash. Then all was dark. Ro fell to the ground in a heap.

The young Klingons seemed happy with their food and their flashlights. It had been nearly four hours since the *Enterprise* had left orbit. Things appeared to be going all right.

Night was falling, and the young Klingons had gathered around Worf at the top of the mound. He was explaining that the time had come to make peace with the colonists.

"We must march to the village tomorrow," he said firmly. "We will tell the colonists what we want. For example, we will insist that this mound and your hutches must be safe. Now think, what else do you want from them?"

"Food!" cried one youngster. The others laughed.

"You want us to go into their hutch?" asked a Klingon teenager. He looked as if Worf had told them to walk off a cliff.

"Yes," said Worf. "The time has come. If you wish to be Klingons and travel in the sky, you must first make peace with the humans in the village."

"If Balak were here, he would say no," the boy said, shaking his head. "The goddess tells us to kill flat-heads. But Worf says we must go to their hutch and make peace. Who is right?"

"Worf!" Wolm cried loudly.

Deanna Troi came forward from the shadows. "You can never go back to your old lives," she explained.

"She speaks the truth," Turrok agreed. "I want to go back to the ship—and fly. I trust Worf. All flat-heads are not bad. Look at Deanna and Data."

The Klingons turned to the two beings who looked human, but were really quite different. Data opened his mouth to explain that he was an android. Worf shot him a look that silenced him.

"You must have your rights," Deanna said. "But killing the settlers is not one of those rights. If you want our help, you must make friends with the settlers. There is no other way."

There was a long silence. "We will go with you to the hutch of the flat-heads," Wolm said.

"Humans," Worf gently corrected.

"Humans," Wolm said. Then she grabbed a drum and began beating it. The others danced for joy.

Worf nodded to Deanna. They slipped away to Data's side.

"We should call Ensign Ro," said the Betazoid. "She can tell the colonists that we are coming."

"I shall tell her that we will arrive tomorrow morning," said Data. He tapped his communicator badge. "Data to Ensign Ro."

There was no answer. He tried again. Still there was no reply.

"Could she be asleep?" asked Deanna.

"This is not her usual sleep period," answered Data. He took out a hand-held communicator. "This was given to me by President Oscaras," he reminded them. "It will put us in touch with the colonists."

Data spoke into the communicator. "Commander Data to New Reykjavik. Come in, please."

After a moment, a voice boomed, "President Oscaras here. Is your party all right?"

"Fine," answered Data. "But we could not reach Ensign Ro on her communicator. Is she well?"

There was silence on the other end. Then a woman's voice came on. "This is Doctor Louise Drayton. Ensign Ro is sleeping. She is sick again from the mantis bite and needs rest. She should be able to return to her duties tomorrow."

"Please give her our good wishes," said Data. "We want to let you know that we will be leading the Klingons to the settlement tomorrow morning."

"What?" cried Oscaras. "You're bringing them *here*?"

"They are coming peacefully," answered Data. "Can you prepare for them? Some food would be a good idea."

Oscaras laughed. "We'll be ready. Don't you worry. We know how much they like food."

Worf added, "We will want to talk. The Klingons have certain demands they wish to make."

"Of course," said Oscaras. "Yes, indeed! We'll be ready for them. Bring them on in!"

Myra sat in her closet on a pile of dirty clothes. She knew that somebody would be coming to the apartment, but she didn't know if it would be her father, Ensign Ro, or people sent by President Oscaras. She had a feeling she should hide.

Just as she was nodding off to sleep, she heard the latch turning. The door banged open. Myra held her breath. She could just make out the voices of two men as they tromped through the apartment.

"Is she here?"

"Doesn't seem to be."

"Well, what harm can a little girl cause? In a few hours, it will all be over."

"Let's report back."

Myra heard the men slam the door shut behind them. She let out a long sigh of relief. Then she crawled out of the closet.

Her dad and Ro were not coming back tonight. They were in real trouble, and there was no one she could turn to for help.

Myra sank down on her bed. The old blankets felt soft. The frightened girl fell sound asleep.

Ensign Ro woke up in a locked storeroom. Her head hurt every time she moved. She looked around and saw Gregg Calvert lying against the metal wall. His head rested on a pile of rags. He was not moving, and his eyes were closed.

Ro blinked. That must have been a heavy stun she had taken. She felt for her communicator badge. It was gone.

That's not surprising, she said to herself. She checked her pocket and found that her phaser was gone, too. She heard the sound of drums far away.

Ro pulled herself to her feet. She tried the only door.

It was locked.

"Hey!" she yelled, pounding on the door. "Let me out! Let me out right now!"

"Shut up in there!" called a voice.

Ro didn't want to give the guard any reason to come closer. She went to Gregg's side and knelt down. She tried to wipe the blood from his face with one of the rags.

Gregg's lips moved. He groaned.

"It's all right, Gregg," whispered Ro. "We're alive. Just rest."

The big man lay back in her arms. She stroked his hair. He tried to smile.

"I take it we lost the fight," he gasped.

Ro nodded. "We're locked up in some kind of storeroom. No windows. One door."

Suddenly Gregg sat up straight. "Myra!" he cried.

"Listen," Ro said, "we're in no shape to help Myra or anyone else at the moment. You don't really think they would hurt her, do you? Now, how do we get out of here? There's at least one guard beyond that door."

Gregg looked around their prison. "The door leads into a hallway. There are rooms like this one on the other side of the walls. These places were put up quickly. It would probably be easier to go through a wall than the door. We'll bend the wall outward from the bottom," said Gregg. "We'll bend it up just enough to crawl under. We can use these rags to protect our hands."

Ro and Gregg wrapped their hands in the rags. They gripped the bottom of the sheet metal. The sharp edge of the wall cut through the rags into their skin. Still, they pulled with all their might, slowly ripping the metal seam.

"Stop," panted Gregg. "I want to see what we're breaking into." He lay down flat and peeked into the darkness beyond.

"Another storeroom," he breathed. "No people."

They began pulling again. They grunted and sweated until the gap was big enough for them to pass under. They crawled out into another storeroom. This one held cleaning tools. Gregg tried the door. It wasn't locked.

"Grab some buckets or mops," he said. "We'll look like we belong. If we see anyone out there, just turn and walk in the other direction."

"Okay," Ro nodded. She grabbed a mop. Then she looked around for something that might make a weapon. Her hand landed on a spray bottle filled with what smelled like strong cleaning fluid.

Gregg took some towels and a bucket. He carefully opened the door and stepped out. The hall was empty.

They walked quickly until they found a door that led outside.

Gregg pointed to a side street, and Ro quickly followed him. They left their buckets and mops in a dark corner. Ro kept the spray bottle.

Darting from shadow to shadow, Ro and Gregg made their way to the Calvert apartment.

"Daddy," said a small voice when they were inside. They saw Myra in the doorway of her room. She was rubbing the sleep from her eyes.

"Honey!" cried Gregg. He picked the girl up and held her tight. She wrapped her arms around his neck.

"They came to get me," Myra gasped, "but I hid.

Daddy, what happened to your head? What's going on?"

"I can't explain now, honey," answered Gregg. "We can't stay here."

"They'll never let us near the radio," said Ro. "We've got to get out of the settlement and find the away team."

"Right," sighed Gregg. He thought a moment. "There's only one person who knows how to get past the guards and the wall."

"Who?" asked Myra.

"Whoever the spy is."

"Do you know who it is?" asked Ro.

Gregg nodded. "I think so. Even if I'm wrong, it will be a good hiding place. It's the last place they would look for us. And it's close."

He reached into a drawer. "Master keys," he said with a smile. "They're from my days as Security Chief. Come on."

Ro, Gregg, and Myra tried to look natural in the streets of the settlement. People were rushing about. They seemed to be getting ready for something. Three more people in a hurry didn't seem strange. Gregg led them to a dark doorway.

As he got out his keys, Ro read the name on the door. "Louise Drayton," the sign said.

Gregg unlocked the door, and they slipped inside the empty apartment. He pulled down the window shade and turned on one light. Then he began moving the bed, couch, and other furniture. He was looking for something on the floor.

"How do you know Drayton is the spy?" asked Ro.

"I first wondered about her when we were aboard your ship," answered Gregg. "Remember when we questioned that Klingon who saved our lives on the beach? He said something about Balak. I asked who Balak was. Drayton jumped right in and answered that he was their leader. How did she know that?"

Ro nodded. Gregg was right.

"Then Drayton turned on us outside the radio room. I knew I was right about her when she ordered that your communicator be taken away." He sank down on his knees and ran his hands over the floor. "Now where is it? It's got to be here."

"What are you looking for?" asked Myra.

The only other room in the tiny apartment was the bathroom. Gregg Calvert went into it. Myra and Ro followed. Gregg grabbed hold of an ugly brown carpet. He peeled it back. Under the rug, resting on the floor, was a metal plate.

"That's it!" exclaimed Gregg. He grabbed the piece of sheet metal and threw it off. There was a big, black hole underneath.

"Wow!" gasped Myra. "A tunnel!"

Gregg got down on his knees and peered into the dark hole. "There's a ladder and what looks like a lantern and some other things."

Gregg looked up at Ro. "She's been trying to destroy New Reykjavik by pitting the Klingons and the colonists against each other. But why?"

Ro frowned. "So both the Federation and the Klingons will clear out. That would leave Selva to the Romulans."

They stood in silence for a few seconds. They were so quiet that they could hear the latch turning on the outside door. Ro waved them back into the bathroom and pulled the door shut.

"What's this?" cried Louise Drayton's voice. "What happened to my furniture?"

Ro decided to act quickly. She stepped out of the bathroom, one hand behind her back.

"Hi!" said the Bajoran cheerfully.

Drayton gasped with surprise. Then a smile crossed her smooth face. Smooth, thought Ro, thanks to the plastic surgery that had turned her from a Romulan into a human.

"Aren't you the bold one?" Drayton said. "I think I'll go tell President Oscaras you're here."

"Please do," replied Ro. "I've got something to show him in the bathroom."

That wiped the smile off Louise Drayton's face. She started to reach into her pocket, but Ro was ready. The ensign pulled the spray bottle from behind her back. Quickly she shot a burning stream of cleaning fluid into the spy's face.

Drayton screamed. She stepped backward, grabbing her eyes. Ro charged across the room and smashed her fist into the doctor's face. Then Ro quickly grabbed the phaser from Drayton's pocket and pointed it at her.

"Where's my communicator badge?" Ro demanded.

"Oscaras has it," Drayton gasped.

"Don't move," warned Ro. "Knowing you, this phaser is set to kill." She checked. It was, indeed, set to kill.

She changed the setting to heavy stun.

Gregg and Myra stepped out of the bathroom. "What is Oscaras up to?" Gregg asked the woman.

"You don't know?" Drayton seemed surprised. Suddenly she jumped to her feet. She dashed for the door. Ro did not wait an instant. She stunned her with a phaser beam. Louise Drayton fell.

"She'll be out at least an hour," said Ro.

Gregg pointed to the bathroom. "There's our way out," he said. "Do you want to take it?"

"We have to," answered Ro. "But let's take her with us."

Gregg Calvert was the first to lower himself into the tunnel. "This lantern will be useful," he called up, "and here is her goddess costume. There's also some kind of whip." He handed it up to Ro. She curled it up and stuck it into her belt next to Louise Drayton's phaser.

Ro handed Drayton's limp body down to Gregg. Then Ro turned off the apartment light. First Myra and then Ro climbed down into the dark hole.

There was no way to pull both the metal plate and the carpet over their heads. Ro decided to cover the hole with only the carpet. If somebody walked into the bathroom, he or she would get a surprise.

She could see Gregg and Myra in the dim light of the lantern. The body of Doctor Drayton lay across Gregg's arms. The tunnel had not been dug. Its smooth walls had been cut out by a phaser.

"Myra," Gregg said in the darkness, "can you pick up the lantern and lead the way?"

"Sure, Dad!" said the girl. "This is cool!"

With the rising sun, the party of twenty-one Klingons, a Betazoid, and an android tramped through the forest toward the settlement.

"Be brave," Worf told the Klingons. "Klingons hold up their heads and do not look afraid."

They continued forward. A man waved from the tower beside the gate. "I'm opening the gate!" he called. "Just step forward, single file."

Worf took the lead. Wolm and Turrok fell in behind him. The others followed. Deanna found herself with Data at the back of the line.

Worf had already passed through the door. The young Klingons were following. It was too late to turn back.

Deanna and Data passed through the gate. It clanged shut. The courtyard was empty. Finally a party led by President Oscaras appeared at one end of the square.

"Welcome!" called Oscaras. He did not move closer. "Is this all of them?"

"Yes," answered Worf. He stood before the huddled youngsters. "I promised them food."

"Of course!" said Oscaras. "Thank you for bringing them here, Lieutenant Worf. You saved us a lot of trouble." Then he raised his arm over his head and shouted, "*Fire!*"

At once colonists appeared in every tower. Others poked their heads from behind buildings. They aimed phaser rifles and fired. Blue beams streaked across the courtyard.

"You lied to us!" screamed a Klingon boy. He drew his knife and leapt at Worf, but a beam cut him down. The lieutenant growled and started to draw his own phaser. Then Worf was blasted. He fell lifelessly to the ground.

Deanna was frozen in shock. The youngsters ran in circles, screaming and trying to escape. But the gate was shut. One by one, the young Klingons fell.

Only Data stayed calm. He drew his hand phaser and picked off every guard in the gate tower. Then he threw open the gate, but it was too late. No Klingons were left standing to escape. Deanna made a dash for the open door, but was cut down herself.

Data knew he could do nothing more. So he picked up a phaser rifle in each hand. Then he jumped over the wall. Beams blasted the dirt at his heels, but he reached the forest without harm.

"Data!" called a voice from the trees.

Data turned and looked among the tree trunks. There he saw the worried face of Ensign Ro.

"We must leave this place," said the android to Ro. "The colonists have taken the Klingons, Counselor Troi, and Lieutenant Worf as prisoners."

"So that's what they were up to," muttered Ro. "You talked the Klingons into making peace, and that's what you got in return. Oscaras is as dangerous as a pit mantis."

"I agree," answered Data. "He told us you were in sickbay when you did not answer my call."

Data followed Ro to a clearing. The android found three humans—a blond man, a female child, and a dark-haired woman. The woman's hands and feet were tied. A gag was in her mouth. Ro explained everything they had been through.

Data looked at the dark-haired woman. "So you are the goddess," he said. "I saw you with Balak. You were the cause of much of the fighting."

"No kidding," said Gregg Calvert. "We know she is a spy. Is there any way to find out if she's a Romulan?"

"Yes," answered Data. "Romulans have a tiny bone in their hands that is missing in humans."

Drayton pulled back when Data bent to look at her hand. It took him only a moment to find the extra bone. "She is a Romulan," he declared. "Do you have her displacer?"

"This?" asked Ro. She reached under some leaves and drew out the whip.

"Yes," replied the android, taking the weapon.

Suddenly a beep sounded in his pocket. Data pulled out the communicator Oscaras had given him.

"This is President Oscaras," boomed a voice. "We are in charge of the planet. We ask you to turn yourself in. Also, do you know where Ensign Ro, Gregg and Myra Calvert, and Doctor Drayton are?"

"Yes," answered Data honestly. But that was all the information he would give. "What was the purpose of attacking us?" he asked.

“To put the Klingons on trial,” said Oscaras.

“For what crime?”

“Murder. We expect to hang them.”

“Do you know,” the android said, “that capital punishment is forbidden in the Federation?”

“Yes,” answered Oscaras. “We expect to withdraw from the Federation.”

“I see,” said Data. “You have no reason to keep Counselor Troi and Lieutenant Worf in prison. I ask that you let them go.”

“When the trial is over,” Oscaras agreed.

Gregg Calvert tapped Data’s arm. He took the communicator. “This is Calvert,” he said.

“Gregg!” roared Oscaras. “Come back to us. You should be here with us, not working against us.”

“Oscaras,” muttered the blond man, “I used to respect you. Now I see you are a fool. Let them all go. You are going to destroy everything.”

“I am in charge of Selva,” growled the president. “I shall make this planet a heaven.”

“By hanging a bunch of children? By going against the whole Federation?” Gregg shook his head. “The *Enterprise* will be back. You can’t keep this a secret.”

“If you don’t return to us, Calvert, I’ll come out there and get you myself!” shouted Oscaras.

“Come and get us. You couldn’t find your nose with your finger!” Gregg snapped the communicator shut.

Myra laughed, but Data asked, “Was it wise to anger him?”

“Yes, it was,” answered Gregg. “I want him to lead a large party out to find us. That way, we can go in there and free your people and the Klingons."

"How will we do that?" asked Data.

"The same way we escaped," answered Calvert. He bent down and threw open the trapdoor that led to Drayton's tunnel. "We have our own entrance."

Worf awoke to find his hands and legs tied. He was on the floor in somebody's quarters. Deanna, lying on a bed, was also tied. "Counselor Troi!" he called.

She moaned as she came to. "Worf," she groaned. "We made a bad mistake. It was a trick."

"They call *us* savages," Worf growled. "The settlers never wanted peace. I do not know where Turrok and the others are. They may be dead." He began to yell, "Let us go! I *demand* it!"

The door opened. President Oscaras walked in, followed by a man with a phaser rifle. "You are in no position to demand anything," he said.

"What are you going to do now?" asked Deanna.

"There will be a murder trial," answered the president. We want to take care of everything before the *Enterprise* returns. But first we have to find Ensign Ro, Commander Data, and the others who escaped. I'm afraid you will both have to stay tied until we return."

"Are you going to kill the children?" asked Worf.

"Yes, Mister Worf, we will hang them. It's kinder than what they did to many of our people."

"But they were coming here to make peace!" cried Deanna.

"We shall have peace," said Oscaras. He turned to

the man with the rifle. "Now, let's find the rest of them."

Deanna heard the door being locked. As Worf pulled on his ropes, he said, "If they kill the Klingon children, it means they will have to kill us, too. They can't let us tell Captain Picard what happened."

Deanna Troi joined Lieutenant Worf in fighting the ropes that tied her arms and legs.

Data hid behind a log. He watched the gate open and a group of armed colonists file out lead by Oscaras.

Data hurried back to the tunnel entrance. "They have come out," he said. "We must be quick."

Soon Ro, Data, and Gregg and Myra Calvert were together in the dark tunnel. Louise Drayton lay tied up on the muddy floor. Myra nervously pointed a hand phaser at the woman.

"Myra," said her father, "I've shown you how to use the phaser. If Doctor Drayton tries to escape, stun her. Stay down here, out of sight."

"Yes, Daddy." The girl nodded. She watched her father, Data, and Ro move off into the dark tunnel. Their voices echoed then faded away.

Ro fingered the new communicator badge as she walked. Data had given one to each of them.

When they came to the ladder at the end of the tunnel, Data climbed up first. Ro and Gregg strapped their phaser rifles to their backs and followed. A moment later, they were standing in Louise Drayton's apartment.

"Phasers on stun," ordered Data.

The android opened the apartment door, and they stepped into the streets of New Reykjavik.

A woman was just walking past. Gregg quickly reached out and pulled her up against the building.

"We don't want to hurt you," said Gregg. "Where are they keeping the prisoners?"

The woman did not answer. Gregg pushed the phaser rifle against her back. She pointed a shaking finger toward a large building. "They're using the dining hall as a jail," she said. "The crew members are in Tony's quarters."

Gregg ordered, "Get to your house and stay there." The woman didn't have to be told twice.

"Data and I will free the prisoners," Gregg told Ro. "You get to the guard tower and keep the gate closed in case Oscaras comes back."

"Signal me when you're ready to leave," said Ro. "I'll meet you back here."

The Bajoran ran in the direction of the gate.

"The Klingons know me," Data said to Gregg. "You go get Worf and Deanna."

Gregg nodded. He dashed in another direction.

Data strode to the door of the dining hall. He smashed it open with one kick. He was hit by a blue beam, but the stun setting did not hurt him. Before the guards saw they were dealing with an android, Data had dropped them with his own phaser.

The young Klingons, tied to table legs, stared in surprise. "Data!" screamed Wolm.

Data snapped the heavy ropes that tied the

youngsters' hands and feet. "Please do as I say," said the android. "We will escape unharmed."

After stunning several surprised guards, Gregg found Deanna and Worf lying back-to-back on the floor. They were trying to free each other's hands.

"We demand to be released!" yelled Worf. He thought Gregg was just another colonist guard.

"No problem," said Gregg. "That's what I'm here for. Data is freeing the Klingons. Ro is guarding the gate."

Deanna blinked. "You're here to rescue us?"

Gregg nodded. "Take these," he said. As Worf and Deanna got to their feet, he handed each of them a communicator badge.

Worf quickly used his. "Worf to Data."

"Data here," came the answer. "I assume you have been freed. Follow Mister Calvert to the tunnel. He planned this escape."

Worf grinned. "With pleasure."

Ro crouched in the tower by the gate. Suddenly a phaser beam ripped by her. Another hit the metal roof. It showered her with hot steel. Ro screamed as flying metal cut her shoulder. Oscaras and his men were back, and they weren't shooting to stun.

Holding her bleeding shoulder, Ro dashed to Louise Drayton's apartment. "Get out of here! Oscaras is breaking through the gate," she shouted at Data and the band of Klingons who waited by the door. She was happy to see Worf and Deanna coming closer.

"Are you not coming?" asked Worf.

Ro shook her head. "I'm wounded. Besides, someone should stay and try to contact the *Enterprise*."

"I'll stay with her," Deanna said to Worf. "Go protect the children."

"We'll put down our weapons," Ro said. "They won't hurt us. Go on now."

There was no time to argue. Gregg and Worf led the young Klingons into the tunnel.

When the tunnel was hidden again, Ro tossed her rifle to the ground. Deanna did the same.

"Lie down," ordered Deanna. "I want to stop that bleeding."

The Bajoran did as she was told. There was more shouting and footsteps. Ro blacked out before Oscaras and his people reached them.

Ro awoke to find herself, once again, in the colonists' sickbay. Deanna Troi sat by her side.

Ro stood. She leaned on the table for a moment, then grabbed Deanna's arm. "Let's get to the lab," she said. "I need to check my equipment."

The shaking began just as Deanna and Ro walked through the laboratory door. Then the alarm on the lab equipment began to blast. The earthquake had barely rattled the windows in New Reykjavik, but crazy lines were streaking across the instrument panels.

"It's happened," Ro gasped. "The tsunami."

Doctor Drayton stared wild-eyed at the Klingons who circled her. She tried to speak through her gag.

They were hidden in a hutch near the settlement. Worf guarded the entrance, and Data waited inside. He thought about their next move. They had to be ready to move quickly, and Louise Drayton was going to be no help in that area. It had been trouble enough carrying her struggling body to the hutch.

"I believe we must return Doctor Drayton to the settlement," the android said to Gregg Calvert.

Data took out his communicator. "Commander Data to New Reykjavik."

A woman's voice answered. "Yes?"

"Please let President Oscaras know that we are returning Louise Drayton. She is a Romulan spy. The proof is the tunnel she dug in her quarters."

Worf held Drayton tightly by the arm. He steered her through the dark forest toward the settlement. Drayton's gag had been removed. "Don't turn me over to the settlers," she begged Worf. "I'll be your friend. I'll help you beat them."

The Klingon frowned. "You sound more like a Romulan all the time. Be quiet!"

They were near the settlement gate now. Worf put his hand over Drayton's mouth. "If you call out, you'll get what a Romulan deserves. When I untie your hands, walk right toward those guards. Speak only to state your name. Now, get going." He pushed Louise Drayton into the clearing.

At first, the woman did just as she had been told. Then suddenly she dropped to her knees. She pointed behind her. "Klingons!" she shouted. "A hundred of them. They're going to attack!"

The colonists began to fire wildly into the forest. Worf was forced to drop to the ground. He could see Drayton rushing into another part of the forest.

Worf knew it was useless to go after her. He would never find her in the black of the Selvan woods. Drayton had escaped.

Captain Picard sat restlessly in an Aretian meeting room. A voice sounded on his communicator. "*Enterprise* to Picard. Captain, I have a subspace call from Ensign Ro."

"Patch her through," replied Picard.

Ro's usually steady voice sounded upset. "I have bad news, Captain," she began. "There has been an earthquake in the ocean. A tsunami is headed our way. The tidal wave is forty meters high. It's moving fast and should reach us in about two and a half hours. We have that long to—well, probably to live."

"A tsunami!" Picard shook off the shock. "You must take cover. You must get out of there!"

Ro sighed. "We have no transporter. We couldn't walk far enough in the short time we have. Also, there's no high ground. But we'll try something, I'm sure. I must end this call now."

Picard tried to think of something to say. "We are on our way," he promised. Within moments, he had transported back to the *Enterprise*. He gave orders for the ship to return to Selva immediately.

Raul Oscaras glared at Ensign Ro. "You're sure about this?" he muttered.

"Check my instruments yourself," she snapped. "We're done playing games. You and the Klingons couldn't live together, but you're going to die together. These buildings won't stand up in a tidal wave. If we only had some high ground—"

"I don't know if it's high enough," broke in Deanna Troi, "but I know the highest ground in the forest. It's a mound built by the Klingons. It's only about an hour's walk from here."

"Give me back my communicator badge," Ro ordered Oscaras. She tapped it and said, "Ro to Data."

"Data here."

"Commander," Ro began, "the *Enterprise* is on its way back. But we have a serious problem. In about two and a half hours we're going to be hit by a tsunami. Counselor Troi says you know of a mound that's the highest point around. We expect to reach there in slightly over one hour. Sir, if you have a better idea, I would be willing to listen to it."

"I felt the quake," said the android calmly. "I believe your course of action is the best one. There is room for everyone to stand atop the mound. However, I believe it is unlikely that many will survive the tidal wave. We will meet you at the mound. We will beat drums to guide you."

"Thank you. Ro out."

"I'll make a broadcast over the settlement loudspeakers," said Oscaras. "I'll have everyone at the main gate in ten minutes."

"No phasers!" warned Ro.

"No phasers," agreed Oscaras. "Let's move."

The line of about two hundred colonists snaked onward. They marched to the beat of drums. Finally, the marchers entered the clearing that circled the great oval mound.

Deanna saw Worf and Data coming toward them, leaving the band of Klingons atop the mound. Ensign Ro hurried forward to meet a young girl and the handsome, blond man who had rescued them.

"How bad is this?" Worf asked Deanna.

Deanna paused before she answered. "Ro says that in about one hour and fifteen minutes a wave as tall as these trees will crash through here."

"How can we withstand that," Worf whispered, "out in the open?"

"We cannot," answered Data. "I think it unlikely that many humanoids will survive. I put my own chances at less than thirty percent."

Deanna noticed that one of the Klingons had rushed down the hill to Worf's side. It was Wolm. She pulled on Worf's jacket.

"Listen to me," Wolm panted. "A giant wave cannot wash us away if we are inside."

Deanna followed Wolm, who led the away team to a clump of dirt at the side of the mound. The Klingon girl began to dig in the dirt with her hands. "We had to hide it," she explained, "long ago when the flat-heads came. We covered it with dirt. It's the old place—home for our dead."

Worf dropped to his knees and began to dig alongside Wolm. Everyone gasped as the dirt fell away to show silver metal.

"It is their ship," whispered Worf.

Data, Worf, and Deanna waved everyone back. Wolm turned the wheel on the hatch. Turrok came to help her. Between the two of them, they got the hatch open. A rush of bad-smelling air poured out.

Data, who was not bothered by the smell, entered the hatch. He came out carrying the rotting body of Balak. He made more trips. Each time he carried out a body. Finally Data came out with a full-grown Klingon skeleton. Deanna knew that it must have been the pilot of the ship.

"That is the last of the bodies," Data said. "The only part of the ship that appears strong enough to protect us is the bridge. It will be tight, but I believe it will hold all of us."

Klingons and colonists alike began streaming through the hatch into the old ship.

They were crammed shoulder to shoulder on the ship's bridge. All past fights were forgotten. They were in this together.

Worf pushed two more colonists through the hatch. He wasn't looking forward to going inside himself—until he heard the noise. It was a dull, horrifying roar. Worf tossed the last of the colonists into the tiny hatch.

The ground shook. The Klingon never moved faster as he leapt through the hatch and spun the wheel shut behind him. He braced himself against the wheel, daring the wave to rip the hatch open.

Just then Louise Drayton came screaming out of the forest. She had waited too long! The Romulan saw the wave rise above her like a blanket about to cover a sleeping child. She knew it was the last thing she would ever see.

The monster wave crashed over the ship, tearing it from the mound. Screaming colonists and Klingons were thrown on top of one another. Leaks showered the frightened passengers. Awful creaking noises nearly drowned out their screams.

"Troi to Data!" shouted Deanna over the android's communicator. "Water is coming in the hatch. I don't think it's going to hold."

"On my way," replied Data calmly.

He found Worf, Deanna, and Raul Oscaras all pushing

frantically against the hatch. Water was leaking in on all sides.

"The seals have rotted," gasped Oscaras. "It's going to blow."

"Perhaps not," answered Data. He reached to his belt and pulled out a black whip. His hand moved on the grip and the green tip began to glow.

"What is that?" growled Oscaras.

"A displacer," answered Data. "Stand aside."

Data snapped the displacer toward the hatch. The water pulled back.

"It changes the air pressure," Data explained.

In movements almost too fast to see, Data turned the handle. He gave a stream of commands to the whip, then cracked it over his head. He let go of the handle, and the whip wrapped around the edges of the hatch. The displacer throbbed for a moment. Then it settled into place where the rotted seal should have been. The flow of water stopped.

The android stepped back. "It should hold."

"I bet you've been practicing with that thing," Deanna said, still shaking.

"For almost an hour," replied Data.

Suddenly the ship bucked like a wild horse. The metal walls groaned.

"I'm afraid the bridge is going to flood," Data said.

Captain Picard jumped to his feet as soon as the gray

planet came into view. “Try to raise New Reykjavik,” he ordered.

“I’m sorry, sir,” answered an officer. “Sensors show that the area is underwater.”

“How soon before we are in communicator range?”

“Ten seconds.”

Picard walked up and down as the seconds passed. Then he hit his communicator badge. “Picard to away team. Come in.” He held his breath.

“Data here,” answered the calm voice. “We are glad you have returned. Two hundred and twenty-eight are accounted for. There are a few injuries.”

“Where are you? How did you—” began Picard. “Never mind. Should we beam you aboard?”

“The sooner the better,” answered Data. “We are up to our knees in water.”

“Transporter rooms stand by,” barked Picard.

A cheer went up from all those standing around Data. Deanna could see humans and Klingons shaking hands and slapping one another on the back. Then they began to disappear in beams of light.

Twenty-four hours later, Ensign Ro and Myra Calvert were sharing a root beer float in the Ten-Forward lounge. Guinan, who was seated across from them, was full of questions.

“What happened next?” asked Guinan.

“We never found the body of Louise Drayton, or whoever she was,” explained Ro. “If the Klingons hadn’t kept that old ship together, you’d still be looking for all of us.”

“Some of the colonists are going back,” said Myra. “but my dad and I have had enough adventure for a while. It’s back to Earth and maybe Starfleet Academy in a few years.”

“What about the Klingons?” asked Guinan.

“Most are going to stay,” answered Myra. “They will rebuild side by side with the colonists. There is a lot they can show one another.”

Ro added, “Two of the younger ones, Wolm and Turrok, decided to join a Klingon ship. They want to learn what they can from the Klingon empire before they return home to Selva.”

Guinan smiled. “I’m glad you’re back, Ro.”

“You were right,” replied the Bajoran. “They needed me down there.”

“That’s all anyone wants,” said Guinan, “to feel needed.”